THE WOMEN OF EZE

BY

SAM ASINUGO

A division of Trident Media Company
801 N Pitt Street, Suite 123
Alexandria, VA 22314 USA

Cover Design
by
Obinna Onyemezikeya

Dedication

This novel is dedicated to all foreigners who gave their lives to Africa in their efforts to achieve peace in the area. You will never be forgotten. And to the young British doctors and nurses who were at St. Mary's Hospital in Amaigbo, Nigeria, between 1962 and 1966. Though I was too young at the time to know your names, I realize the great value of your service. Thank you for taking care of so many children who would have otherwise perished. Love knows no color and friendship has more end in view than any other object of desire.

To my mother, Juliana and my father, Israel Asinugo who told me the story of Neka, my grandfather's second wife. But most importantly, for their faith, love and support they freely gave me over the years. Also to my wife Liz and my children, Ian, Nigel and Olivia. You have a special place in my heart.

Many thanks to Trish Bozell, my editor, both for her friendship and for believing in me as a novelist.

Chapter 1

May 1981
First Day

A fog rose gradually from the rushing waterfall, while several streams raced through the gorges that fed the lake. The surrounding hills were full of green branches, and the forest air was laden with the poignant aroma of wild roses, African water lilies, and the lighter scent of southern grasses. The fog permeated the tree canopies, filling the morning air with freshness. I can't remember a fresher morning. The joyful rays of the new day had not reached into the gorge, but a gentle puff of wind showered us with silver dew from the thick leafy bushes that grew in the deep folds of the cliffs. Under the thickness of the mist, birds sang in the trees as if beckoning the sun to appear. Suddenly, the forest froze with an eerie quiet. Even the birds stopped singing. The painful cries of young girls echoed over the hills, almost drowned by the roaring torrents of the waterfall. Their wails grew closer and closer as we walked on.

It was seventeen years ago in the town of Eze, in eastern Nigeria. Their voices were like mine, like an eight-year-old's. As we walked, a slight rustle in the forest sent numbing fear through my heart. I clasped my hands around my mother's wrist as we approached a red clay-walled hut. The wooden doors creaked open. My eyes fell on bloodied terror. Ten children writhed in pain. Some lay on the floor crying, while others chanted, adding to the tumult. Still others lay silent, as if in shock. A chill went through my heart, and tears fell down my cheeks. My body was frozen with fear, my lips dry and trembling. I looked at my mother, but no explanation was forthcoming. She too, was crying. My breath rushed out as two hands grabbed me. I screamed. Two old women glared into my eyes. When I looked back an instant later, my mother had vanished. Paralyzed with fear, I felt the warmth of urine running down the inside of my thighs. Struggling and kicking, I was dragged farther into the inner chamber of the hut.

"Be quiet, Nina," a voice sounded behind a dirty white curtain.

The curtain drew open. I immediately recognized Ada, the chief sorceress. She stood taller than everyone around her. She was dressed in traditional wrappers, her plaited hair reaching upward like radio antennae. My nose twitched as it caught a whiff of her binta perfume. It was the scent that hung around the dead during burial ceremonies--the scent of a woman gone bad.

"Today, Nina, you will be circumcised," Ada said. "I will prepare you for the passage into womanhood according to the wishes of our great-grandfathers. You will make your father proud. He will be honored to offer your hand in marriage when you come of age."

My mouth opened, but my words caught in my throat as the six women lifted me off my feet. I was carried behind an old white curtain, pinned down on a mat made of palm frond. I kicked and fought to break free, but their grips were vice-like.

My urine-stained underwear was quickly pulled from my waist. Struggling against the strength of the women, I tried to roll on my stomach, but it was impossible. My legs were violently held ajar. An old bowl filled with water was placed on a wooden stand next to Ada. A red substance floated in the water, probably blood from Ada's previous victims. Her hand groped through the bowl and emerged with a rusty dagger.

"Keep her still!" she commanded.

I screamed as the first cut sent a searing pain through my spine, then radiated into my hands and feet.

"You're going to kill me," I shouted, and then began to plead. But Ada was impervious to my pain. Her wrist rose and fell in an even rhythm as she cut at my clitoris. Overwhelmed with pain, I shut my eyes tightly and clenched my teeth. Blood flowed softly between my buttocks, warm to my senses. My body quivered with pain, and for several minutes the hut seemed to reel around me.

For a moment I opened my eyes slightly, and saw Ada with something else. It was a smaller dagger, which she had placed over a burning log in an old fireplace. She dropped some oil on the dagger, and blue smoke rose in the air. Gently, she dropped the hot oil on the tissue which she had cut. Another wave of pain shot through my body. My brain felt as if it were on fire, and my lungs grew heavy.

"You have to hold her still!" Ada scolded. "If I don't get the hot oil in her, her wounds won't heal, and she will become infected."

As more oil dropped, I was numbed by the pain. A cloud descended over me, guiding me into the realms of unconsciousness from which I sought peace--never wanting to wake--begging to be lifted into the hands of the Great Ruler of all things.

*   *   *

"I'm sorry, Princess. I had to do it or no man would marry you."

I opened my eyes. My mother was sitting on the mat next to me. She was running her hand across my forehead. She, too, had tears in her eyes and her lips fluttered. I could tell from the orange rays of the sun that shone through the tiny window that several hours had passed. My body was frozen with pain, and my vulva felt raw. Children were still crying in the outer chamber of the hut. Occasionally, the sound of adult conversation would rise over their clamor.

For the first time, I began to notice my surroundings. On the far corner of the hut was a pile of dirty laundry. An old kerosene-operated refrigerator flanked the doorway to the right. A spider dangled on its thread over my head, its web slung over a crossbeam that supported the corrugated iron roof.

My hand tightened around my mother's wrist. "I want to go home to Papa." My voice was guarded.

"Your father has left for Port Harcourt. He won't be home for two weeks. I'm afraid you have to be here until you are properly healed."

"For how long, Mama?" Just then, another child was

8

placed on the mat to my right. She didn't move or speak.

"You must leave now."

I turned to the voice, it was Ada. I clung to my mother's wrist. "Please don't leave me, Mama." But mother, too, feared Ada. She reluctantly rose to her feet. I was distraught to see her leave. I felt empty. I was left alone with my own pain. Not even my father who was regarded as the strongest man in the whole town could save me now.

"What's your name?" the girl next to me asked weakly.

Gradually, I lifted my body to face her.

"I'm Nina," I said, and waited for her reply. Then I saw that she lay in a pool of blood. She had mustered only enough strength to ask my name. I began yelling to draw the attention of the adults. But each attempt sent a surge of pain through my body. It was as if my nerves and tendons were being pulled from my brain, out through my arms and legs. Quietly, I began to cry again, and shut my eyes to the sight that only the gods of this land would ever condone.

Finally, the women returned. They began changing the pieces of cloth that were wrapped tightly around the girl's crotch.

"She won't stop bleeding," one of the women complained. They began talking furiously amongst themselves. It was then that I knew vaguely through their conversations that Ada had cut too much, and the girl had hemorrhaged. Her lips were pale and chapped. Her eyes were yellow as if she had jaundice. I had the absurd feeling that the women were as afraid as I.

By the silence of the bushes that surrounded the hut, I could tell it was nightfall. During the day, I would hear the noisy weaver birds in the trees, but now, I only heard an owl.

My attention was riveted to the girl next to me. I was eager to find out her name and make friends. She was in more pain than I. Her eyes had rolled back in her head. My mother once told me this happened to people before they died. I saw a shadow over me. It was Ada. I closed my eyes and pretended to be asleep, wishing this were only a nightmare.

Second Day

When morning came, the girl came around. She immediately began calling for her mother, but the adults weren't around.

"I'm the only one here," I said. "What's your name?"

She said softly, "My name is Chichi, and I'm five. I'm going to die."

"You are not going to die," I said, and began reciting prayers that I had learned in school. I comforted her. And also told her that Ada had promised to make her well, but she shook her head and turned to the wall. She didn't want to die. The day wore on, and during moments of delirium she mumbled about going home to her brothers and sisters. At times she would call her father and mother by affectionate names as tears gushed from her eyes. But at other moments, she chided them for not loving their princess. And for leaving her in the hands of an evil woman. I was only a few years older than Chichi, but I knew death when I saw it.

A few hours later, the women surrounded Chichi. She was sinking back into unconsciousness. She would fade for several hours, and then come around. I couldn't tell if she was breathing. She mumbled words that were unclear. Then, suddenly, she turned and called my name.

"Nina!" her voice rose in pitch.

"I'm here, Chichi."

"Please, don't leave me."

The women heard Chichi's voice and rushed back into

the room.

"I won't." I stared defiantly at the women who were staring down at me.

"Are you a Christian?" Chichi asked.

"Yes."

"So am I," she said. "But my papa is not. I'm afraid our spirits will not be joined in the next world. Our teacher told me."

Within a few minutes, Chichi's body began to shake with cold chills. Her cheeks were sunken and her eyes large. She asked to be placed in the sun but the women refused. I touched her the next moment, and her body burned with fever. When evening came, she was groaning in terrible pain. I stayed up listening to her, offering words of comfort. When the pains let up, she tried to make me believe that she was getting better. An oil lamp burned nearby on an old wooden stand. Through the flickering orange light, I saw tears gleaming in Chichi's eyes. It was the pain of a lost child wishing to be reunited with her mother.

Third Day

Early in the morning, she was quiet and did everything Ada asked her to do. The pieces of cloth that tied her wounds came loose. She began bleeding profusely. Again, the women tied her wounds. She seemed almost fine.

Chichi's mother brought her meals. Her dish was a bowl of akamu, akara, and boiled crested franklin eggs. But Chichi was too weak to eat, and her mother tried to force-feed her.

When afternoon came, Chichi complained of the heat. Her mother opened the window, but it was hotter outside than in. Chichi then asked for water. Her mother helped her with a cup. For several minutes she seemed all right. Moments later, she called out weakly for more water. I felt a stirring within myself and knew Chichi was coming to her final hour. I began saying the same prayer I learned in school. How long I prayed, I do not know. Then, her body suddenly twitched and buckled, as she began bleeding again.

Chichi finally lay peacefully next to me. Ada walked into the room. She had not a single tear in her eyes. She placed a mirror against Chichi's lips, and it didn't mist. She drew a dirty white sheet over Chichi's body, and left the room. An eerie silence fell in the hut. I cried harder, and began shoving Chichi, begging her to wake. When I saw her blood seep through the old white sheet, I broke down altogether. Our bond had become great, and I felt totally helpless. I yearned to hear her voice again.

*   *   *

Much time had passed when I heard Chichi's mother weeping outside. She was being consoled by the other women. I didn't have much sleep. Occasionally, I would drift between sleep and wakefulness. Something strange began happening right before my eyes. The hut seemed to be on fire. A bright beam of light shone over Chichi. Gently, a plume of smoke rose slowly through the light. A tall man dressed in a white robe with a black sash around his waist stood over Chichi's body. Her body was gradually lifted through the smoke and the light into the man's arms. He kissed Chichi's lips and his warmth passed into her. Chichi's body came alive, and she smiled joyously. My words rang with wonder:

> *Our Father, Who art in heaven,*
> *Hallowed be Thy name.*
> *Thy kingdom come, Thy will be done,*
> *on earth as it is done in heaven.*
> *Give us this day our daily bread.*
> *And lead us not into temptation,*
> *but deliver us from evil.*
> *For Thine is the kingdom,*
> *and the power, and the glory,*
> *for ever and ever. Amen.*

Fourth Day

When morning came, I opened my eyes but Chichi was gone. I heard a man's voice outside. It was the only male voice that I had heard since arriving in the hut. Men were forbidden to enter during female circumcision.

I staggered to my feet. My insides felt raw, and the pain radiated from my pelvis into my groin. I began coughing, sending a burning pain through my head and lungs. I held onto the wall to prevent myself from sagging to the floor. Using the wall for support, my steps labored, I staggered to the window. Chichi's body sat upright, bound onto a bicycle carriage supported by two short poles. Her back was turned to the rider because it was a common belief that the dead must ride home backward.

The rider was a short thickset man wearing a black short-sleeved shirt. His shirt was ripped in several places. Signs of a strenuous life could be seen on his wrinkled face. The palm leaves between his lips, which were believed to ward off evil spirits along the way, didn't help his expression. His brows, colored with white chalk, and his neck with red clay, gave him the look of a fierce warrior.

As the man rode away with Chichi's body, a chill went through my heart. Instinctively, I began waving, hoping somehow Chichi would know that I loved her. Though I had only known Chichi for a short time, we had forged an unspoken bond. We promised to be true to our friendship. It was in her eyes, the way she looked at me a few minutes before she died, the way tiny droplets of tears fell from her eyes. We promised always to keep in touch, both in faith and in spirit. I knew that I had lost the most important friend that I would ever have in this world.

A few days later, my mother told me Chichi had been buried in the forest. Her parents were not allowed to bury her in the graveyard of the young because those who died of circumcision were believed to bring a bad omen to the living. Throughout the following days, thoughts of Chichi filled my heart. When I would finally fall asleep, I dreamed the same thoughts that had kept me awake.

Fifth Day

It was early in the morning when I awoke. I stared at the ceiling. A gecko dashed across it in pursuit of a cockroach. The insect ran for dear life, but the gecko caught it. As it chewed on the insect, the wings floated onto my face. Quickly, I got up and shook my face.

I looked to see Ada standing over me. "Where's my mother?" I asked.

Ada turned her head and looked behind her. My mother was standing in the doorway. I rose from the mat and walked shakily toward her. Several pieces of cloth were wrapped around my crotch which made walking difficult.

When I left the hut's inner chamber, all the children whom I had seen at the time I had entered, were gone.

Looking through the small wooden door, I saw a large courtyard that I hadn't noticed before. To my right was a small shrine adorned with several statues of naked gods. One old male and four young females. Feathers were stuck onto the statues, hardened by clots of blood. The foul odors that emanated from the shrine churned my stomach. The ground around it was strewn with eggs and parts of sacrificed chickens.

Ada walked through the door. I tugged on my mother's arm.

"I want you to take me home to Papa." I was afraid of the shrine, and I was angry at my mother for bringing me to such a place.

Thoughts of Chichi rushed through my mind. She had not been buried according to the Christian faith. I wondered whether she would go to heaven. She was buried in the forest of the Haunted Ruins. Only evil people from our town were buried there, including those thought to bring bad luck. These included deformed children, people who committed suicide, and villains. All the children were afraid of this forest.

My mother took my hand and led me through a path in the forest. Each step sent a searing pain through my body. But I continued walking, happy that I had finally left behind Ada's hut and its painful experiences.

*   *   *

My breathing was labored. "I want to take a rest, Mama. I'm tired." My mother cleared a spot in the bush, and I carefully sat down. We were surrounded by three hills. From where we sat, I could hear the waterfalls in the forest.

"Come to me, Princess," my mother said, with her arms outstretched. Her voice was resonant. She took me on her lap. For a moment, I saw in her eyes the mother I'd always known. I wanted to trust her again, believe in her, and make this nightmare go away.

"Do all the girls get circumcised, Mama?"

"Yes."

"Did you...too?" She looked away sharply and pretended not to hear me.

"Did you, Mama?" I asked, and tugged on her blouse. She looked at me sadly, and sighed.

"Almost all the women in our country do," she said

ruefully. "It is our tradition, Christians and Moslems alike."
I was shocked.

"We've lost too many children," she said. "I was afraid you weren't going to make it, Princess."

She continued to run her hand over my forehead.

"Why is the big forest feared by everyone?"

"It is the forest of Alamezie, the forest of the Haunted Ruins." She sighed, and shook her head. Then she looked down at me with a pained smile. "Poor Neka and her little ones. Several bad things happened in that forest and its hills, Nina. It is not a story for a little child."

Painfully, I rose from my mother's lap. "What are you saying, Mama? Neka had children?" I was confused. Neka was the nicest woman in our town. She always brought me udala fruits. I thought she could never have children.

"She had three sets of twins."

"What happened to her children, Mama?"

She looked at me evasively. "It's not your place to know."

"What about Chichi? Why was she buried in this forest? It wasn't her fault! She was never a villain, neither was she deformed or committed suicide. It isn't fair." I began to cry.

"Ada determines what happens in this town," she chided. "She is a powerful sorceress. She sees everything. She even knows when you breathe your desires."

We resumed walking. Several thoughts went through my mind:

> *How does this woman, Ada, control everyone's life? What happened to Neka's children? Was she, too, afraid of Ada? Will Chichi*

remember me?

Two miles later, we passed by the local market. I saw Uloma, the mad girl. She danced naked at her usual spot. My mother once told me Uloma was thirteen. She leaped into the air with agility, displaying her acrobatic dance with athletic skill. She wore a bushy afro, and her dark olive supple skin shone in the morning sun. Occasionally, she would stop to communicate something to herself. She would do a spin, then sing and dance slowly to her own tunes, and gradually resume her acrobatic leaps. Her firm breasts rose and fell gracefully with each jump. Young men were eyeing her. Every passerby stopped to watch. She was a beauty in heart-rending distress.

I kept taking quick looks at Uloma as the market disappeared into the turn, wondering if she was circumcised. Rumors circulated that Uloma's family was cursed by the gods of the forest. Uloma, as a child, had been taken to the forest to be cleansed of her family's curse. It seemed as if no sacrifice to the gods could reverse the curse on her family. Heart-broken and ostracized by our town, Uloma's parents left to live in another town. They weren't permitted by the chief to take Uloma along. It was feared that her departure would bring a plague of disease, since she was the bridge between the oracle of the hills and our town. It was later learned that Uloma's parents died of unknown causes. She was the only living member of her family left. No one cared.

*   *   *

"Good morning, Papa." My thoughts left me as my

father greeted me back in our courtyard. He leaned over me. And I wrapped my arms around his waist, and buried my face in his chest. I cried.

We clung to each other for what seemed like minutes. When I turned, several children from the neighboring houses joined us. Shyly, I hid my face behind my father as he led me into the house, unsure whether the other children knew what had happened to me. My life changed from that moment on. A simple laugh from my friends made me feel uneasy. It was as if everyone was laughing at me.

*   *   *

Later that afternoon, I sat naked on a small stool in our bathroom stall. The stall was made from palm frond. A low pedestal, placed in the middle of the stall, served as a platform for a bucket of water and as a guard against the unpaved surface. Through openings between the palm frond, I could see pedestrians walking through the path in the woods. I found the stall great fun because it had no roof. The intense tropical sun shone over my body, and when it rained, the cool water was exhilarating. I waited for my mother to arrive with her bucket of water. We always enjoyed our baths together.

I had been afraid to look at myself since my circumcision. Gently, I lowered my head and gradually spread my legs. My clitoris and the surrounding tissue had been cut away, my vulva exposed. I heard my mother coming, and quietly rose to my feet. I was ashamed for her to see me in this condition.

"Mama, do you think Uloma, the mad girl, is circumcised?"

"Yes, Nina. Every woman is in this town."

"Why do girls get circumcised?" I looked at my mother expectantly. She was reluctant to discuss sex.

"So you don't become a harlot," she responded. "Your mind should be focused only on your husband. Your obligation to our great-grandfathers is to make your husband happy, farm the land, raise his children--nothing else. Many of our girls have run away to big cities, and are now prostitutes. They run around in mini skirts and trousers. It is the fault of the foreigners. No one wants to see his children end up in that fashion."

"If that's true, Mama, how come I heard you tell Neka that it hurts when Papa puts his thing in you? I even heard you say that it was because of circumcision." My mother was shocked. She gazed at the surrounding palm frond, contemplating her answer.

"What's an orgasm, Mama? I heard you say that you've never had one in your life. You weren't too happy when you said it. Circumcision must not be that great after all!"

"Quiet, Nina! That's not the way to talk to your mother."

Embarrassed, my mother quickly began washing herself. She refused to meet my gaze. I sat on the stool looking at her fixedly, trying to find some resemblance between my surgery and hers. And I knew that she watched me from the corner of her eyes as if she were cross-eyed. I was angry.

"You had that stinky sorceress circumcise me and all you can tell me is to be quiet? I can't even bend over to take a bath, Mama. My nerves seem to be pulled from my body. I can't even cough without shaking with pain."

"Keep your voice down, Nina. A word in the wrong

place, and your father will be fined by the town for talking ill of Ada. People have lost their lands for much less. We have only three fields left, and we don't want to lose them to the chief."

Chapter 2

June 1981

I stood under an iroko tree waiting for Neka's arrival. We usually met at dawn, after she had made her rounds picking udala fruits that had fallen during the night before. I wished Chichi could stand beside me, to enjoy the sweet white syrup from the yellow udala fruit. Her agony at Ada's hut was now clearer in my mind.

I couldn't stop thinking about Uloma, the mad girl who danced naked at the market. Long ago, I saw her at the market, blood crusted on the inside of her thighs. My mother said it happened once a month to every woman. It was a sign of coming of age. Uloma is so beautiful. How could Ada circumcise a mad girl?

"Good morning, Mama," I said, as Neka approached. I always called her Mama, as if she were my own mother. Her walk was naturally elegant; she was tall, dignified, and majestically beautiful. The rich colorful wrapper hung delicately around her supple waist. She wore a buba and a headwrap to match. I saw in her large brown eyes the beauty of youth. She was slightly younger than my mother, and she had a unique way of connecting with children.

"You are far too early, Nina. It's still dark out here. Aren't you afraid of the forest? Three mambas were killed

25

here yesterday." She took furtive looks around her to make sure no snakes still lingered around the iroko tree before she sat down on one of its large roots that projected from the earth.

"I'm not afraid of snakes. My father makes snake soup, which I love." I looked at the woman before me. She was far more beautiful than all the women in our town. Her spirit was untouched. Her smile promised more happiness than all the gods will ever know. I wondered what happened to her six children. Was she resigned to her fate? She handed me some of her udala fruit. She broke one, and sucked on the sweet syrup.

"I heard you've been made a woman," Neka said calmly, looking into space. I thought I saw tears glint in her eyes.

"Yes." My voice lacked its usual enthusiasm, and she took note. "I don't think my parents love me."

"Nonsense, Nina. Your parents love you. Your mother is a wonderful woman. Because of her, I am sitting here with you today."

"Then why did she let Ada cut me so badly? Why did Chichi have to die?"

Neka shook her head, and squeezed my knee reassuringly. "Circumcision is not a journey for a child, my dear Nina. Last year five girls died in this town. I know there is hurt and anger in everyone towards Ada, because some towns in our country have nearly stopped this practice. But no one would dare challenge her. She connived with our chief, and through superstition they have convinced our people to believe that this should remain a normal practice. They have enriched their pockets by charging large fees for circumcising every girl born to a family in this town. Many families who couldn't pay have lost their lands."

She looked at me intently, her eyes stared into mine. She pointed to the sky. Although it was early morning, the first rays of the sun had not reached into the forest. The moon was still up, and it was so large that it seemed God had cut a huge circle of fire and made it into a disk. A lone star flanked the moon to the right, and they seemed to float softly with the clouds.

"Chichi is in heaven now. Not even Ada nor our great-grandfathers can harm her."

"I thought you could never have children. My mother told me you gave birth to sets of twins." Neka sighed and lowered her head.

"I did," she answered pensively, and wouldn't meet my gaze.

"Were they boys or girls?"

"Two boys and four girls. They are now in heaven with Chichi."

"What happened to them?"

"Twins born in our town are sacrificed to the gods of the forest. It was taboo to have twins."

I rose to my feet. "You mean your babies were killed?"

"It's like this, Nina. When a woman is in labor she is taken to Ada's hut. I was only fifteen when my first babies were born. In the back of Ada's house, on an old mat, six women waited for my arrival. My first pregnancy was the hardest. I was in labor for two days. Everyone thought my baby was dead. When the baby finally came, the women around me were elated. They began singing and chanting with joy. As I began to push again, they thought it was the afterbirth, but it was my second baby. As the head came into view, I could see the look of horror in their eyes. And then, one by one, they left.

"I was in shock with pain. My babies were crying. I was bleeding, and my strength was gone. I cried and began calling for my husband, but he didn't come. I knew the news had reached him for he was waiting in the courtyard. He was the only friend that I had. But he left, believing that I had brought shame to his family. The birth of twins could ruin a marriage and friendship forever.

"So, still naked, with blood and birth fluids running from my body, I crawled toward my babies. They were wrapped in an old cloth. I gently unwrapped them, and cradled them in my arms. Immediately, they stopped crying. It was as if they were bonded to me in spirit, but then I was struck with the reality of my predicament. The women returned, and this time they brought Ada with them.

"You can't do anything right!' Ada scolded. Her slap tore across my face. 'You have shamed your family and the gods of this land. Your husband has to appease our gods for what you've done.' My head rang, and little stars danced in front of me. I held my babies tightly against my chest and mustered my strength to prevent myself from sagging to the ground."

My heart hurt as I heard Neka tell her story. "What did you do?" Again, she squeezed my knee reassuringly.

"I hugged my babies tightly against my chest. Then someone came from behind me and held a piece of cloth hard over my nose and mouth. I couldn't breathe. I slumped to the floor. My babies were taken from my arms. When the cloth was lifted, I took a gulp of air. I stood hopeless and helpless as my babies were placed in a red clay pot. I pleaded with the women to at least save one baby, but none of them would look at me.

"It was dark when the women left, and I knew exactly where they were headed. I gathered my strength and went after them quietly as they walked into the forest of the Haunted Ruins. Climbing through the hills and rocks, I hid behind an oilbean tree. Whatever noise I made was drowned by the noise from the waterfall. My heart pounded against my chest as I waited for them to leave."

I rose to my feet. "Weren't you afraid? They say the forest and the hills are filled with skulls of dead people."

"I was afraid, my child. But the bond of blood between my children and I held my sense of being intact. What happened to me would have made others go mad or take their own lives. So there I was, lying low behind the oilbean tree. Suddenly, the sky roared with thunderclaps. Heavy winds shook the tree branches and showered me with dead leaves.

"Through the lightning I could see Ada rocking back and forth in front of a large wooden statue. She was singing and chanting rituals to the gods. After what seemed like hours, they sacrificed a chicken. I heard the wings of the chicken flap as it died. Rain began to clatter with urgency against the forest canopy. The wind broke twigs and branches. One after the other they began to leave, sure that a civet cat and soldier ants would devour my children before dawn."

Neka's face was now pale and tired. I, too, was afraid. I kept looking around the Iroko tree, making sure none of the mambas that thrived in the forest crawled at our feet. The syrup from the udala fruits Neka gave me had leaked between my fingers and had stuck like glue. My stomach churned and my appetite was gone.

"Did you find your babies?"

"Yes. But not once did I hear them cry. I ran to where Ada had sat. The pot was placed between two wooden gods next to a banana tree. When I opened the pot, my babies were limp. A quiet chill went through my heart. I picked up the first baby. She awoke, and began to cry. As if on cue, her sister, too, began crying. Quickly, I laid Rachael down and cupped my hands over their mouths. I was afraid Ada and the other women could catch wind of their cries and would return. I cried silently, wishing everything would be all right. You see, since I had become a Christian, I gave them all Christian names so their spirits would go to heaven."

"What were their names?" Tears gushed from my eyes.

"Let's see... Rachael came first, then Rebecca, Elizabeth, Mary, Joshua, and Samuel."

"What happened after you found them?"

"I broke a leaf from a banana tree, and I used it as a shield against the rain. But the heavy wind rendered it useless. My babies still got wet. Gradually, with the aid of lightning, I began tracing my way through the hills. My husband was my only hope. I wanted him at least to turn the babies over to the new church out of town or run away with me to where twins were not killed. We were both young. We could have done it. As I walked, the flood water along the way was ankle deep. The wind blew across my face, threatening to knock me into the steep and down the rocks. My legs were weak from two days of labor.

"When I got home, I knocked. My husband took a moment to open the door. His face filled with horror. He did not expect to see me. He quickly closed the door in my face. He did not want anything to do with our twins. Frightened, confused, and rejected by my only hope, I sat alone in the courtyard, wet from the rain, and in the darkness of the night. My babies shivered in the cold rain. When morning came, a large crowd had gathered. My babies were hardly moving and their faint cries were nearly inaudible. I too had fallen sick. I could barely hold them in my arms. If my husband had been a Christian..."

Neka's lips quivered as more tears fell quietly down her cheeks. "Did they die?" I looked at Neka uneasily. She seemed to be in a trance. Her eyes were glazed as she stared into the distance. She was absorbed by something in the near forest, something far beyond my sight and imagination. She paused. Moments later, she slowly came around to me.

"This time, Ada made sure they were dead before they were taken back to the forest.

"You see, my husband never married me in the normal way. When I was thirteen years of age, my parents borrowed money from his parents. My father could not repay the money. Therefore, I was indentured to his parents until the money could be repaid. Only two weeks into my servitude, my husband first raped me. I ran from their house to my parents. I told my mother what had happened. She was distraught. But she could tell no one because she knew my father could not repay the money. If I had stayed home, my father's honor would have been at stake. And our lands would have been taken from us. The following day, my mother could do nothing but return me to my husband's parents. She was heartbroken to leave me behind.

"Two days later, my husband raped me for the second time. I told his mother, but she only scuffed me, telling me that I had made it all up. I don't remember how many times I ran from their house, but each time, I was forced to go back. Several times, I tried to commit suicide, but each time I was found and punished for one month for bad behavior. And for almost invoking a curse on the whole town by trying to commit suicide. Once, they believed I had gone insane. They took me to a voodoo doctor to cleanse me of evil spirits. Only my husband knew what was happening to me because he always raped me on the farm, four miles from home. There were no witnesses.

"Once he brought two of his friends. When I saw them, I immediately knew what would happen. I ran without looking back. The two young men chased me through the forest with my husband behind them. It was as if an angel had planted a chetah's sprint in my feet. When I reached my new home, I complained to my husband's mother. She beat me with a cane, and said that I was lazy and didn't want to finish my task. She escorted me back to the farm. I saw my husband hiding behind the bushes. His friends were with him. They waited for his mother to leave. This time, I didn't run. I continued to hoe the ground.

"'Why didn't you run this time?' he asked with a smirk.

"I stopped hoeing and looked at him. He and his friends surrounded me.

"'Would you do this to me if I were your sister?' I asked,

hoping to move him, or at least to have him feel an inner uncertainty.

"Why did you run from me, you bitch?"

"His slap tore against my face, knocking me to the ground. The forest seemed to move in circles around me. One of his friends groped under my gown, and began laughing. They took turns raping me. It seemed I could do nothing but accept my husband, because no one seemed to care.

"I began to turn my mind from the bad side of him, and to view him as the strong man that he was. He continued to rape me until I got pregnant when I was fifteen. He was forced to marry me. So...I began to love him in my own unusual way. But not once did he ever tell me that he loved me. When my father learned that I was pregnant, he was happy because he no longer had to repay the money he owed my husband's parents.

"When my husband died last year, I went home to my mother. My father too, had died. In a way, it was my home-coming. I wanted to be with my childhood friends, but they had all married and were living in distant towns. I wanted to relive the childhood that was taken from me, and leave my painful memories behind. But so many changes had taken place. The first thing I did was hug my mother. She knew what was in my heart. There was an unspoken apology in her eyes. All the people of this town are responsible for what happened to me. They took my children away and sacrificed them to the gods of the forest."

It took me several years to understand the word rape, and the magnitude of Neka's suffering. As a child, the story of her husband was etched in my mind. I was dejected to see Neka so hurt.

She rose to her feet, and beat her buttocks, to loosen the particles of tree barks that had collected on her wrapper. I followed her as she walked to the nearby bush. I was afraid to leave her side. She clipped a leaf from a cocoa-yam plant and wrapped my udala fruits in it.

"I want you to take me to the forest of the Haunted Ruins."

She turned sharply, and looked at me. "It is no place for a child, Nina. Moreover, your mother will be angry if she finds out."

"I promise to tell no one." She met my gaze, and found truth in my eyes.

*   *   *

Dew descended onto the forest from the hillside, shining in the first rays of the morning sun. Moisture on the green vegetation licked our bodies, wetting us. Incessant croaks from crested franklins in the distance created an eerie atmosphere. Hummingbirds sucked on the sweet nectar of wild plants, while other birds harmonized in the trees around us.

We reached a narrow walk. The forest seemed to freeze. An air of solitude pervaded the place. Everything was so mysterious: the murky shade of the forest above the foaming torrents from the waterfall as it roared down from ledge to ledge, cutting its way through the green-clad hills, the ravines full of mist and silence, and the gurgling of small streams as they raced each other through holes in the rocks, before flowing into the huge basin of the lake in the distant valley. The freshness of the scented air, laden with the heavy smell of acacia and southern grasses, compounded a feeling of grandeur and of sadness--something deep within nature of which only the gods of the forest could tell. I looked at a distant rock; an eagle, disturbed by our presence, left its perch and took to the air. A kingfisher sensing the departure of the eagle, resumed fishing. It dove into the water and emerged with a large fish. The fish struggled, but made a perfect cross on the bird's beak.

I clung to Neka's arm as the warning calls from troops of baboons rose in pitch. An occasional rustle on the forest floor sent goose bumps over my body. Neka would stiffen at a rustling of leaves, as animals disturbed by our presence ran from our path. The area was infested with civet cats, mambas, and foot-and-a-half long centipedes.

"How far do we have to walk?" I asked, tugging on Neka's blouse.

"Not much farther, Nina," she said reassuringly, but I sensed her nervousness.

The path opened into a green valley, like a desert oasis. The mist from the lake slowly rose into the air. The silence sent numbing fear through my body. Even the baboons had stopped their warning calls, and the birds their singing. I had the absurd feeling that all the creatures of the forest had stopped to watch in anticipation of what would happen.

Neka paused. She could see the worried look on my face.

My heart beat in my throat. There was a life-sized statue of a man in front of us. At its base were the skulls of several young children. A Caucasian doll stood next to a grave. I

35

wondered what a white person would be doing in a forest in this distant part of the world. Then I remembered that rich Africans bought their children Caucasian dolls because they were the only ones available in supermarkets in the big cities. I hid behind Neka and took furtive looks at the objects around the statue: cowrie shells, rings, and talismans made in the form of pendants. My legs trembled with fear. Given a choice at that moment, I would have run home to my mother.

Neka pointed to a shallow grave next to a large acacia tree. The earth was fresh, though it was slightly eroded by rain.

"That's Chichi's grave. I know that's the reason you came."

Quickly, I ran to the site, unafraid of the ominous statue that stood to my right. I began crying, calling Chichi all the sweet names that my mother had taught me. Neka looked at me, dejected. I knew inwardly she shared my grief. After several minutes, Neka planted a cross. We couldn't tell where Chichi's head rested, but Neka placed the cross at the highest part of the mound. I put some wild flowers there, and placed my udala on the grave. We said a quick prayer and when we opened our eyes, the question spurted from my mouth.

"Are these the skulls of your babies?" Neka was taken aback at my boldness, but she understood the inquisitive mind of a child.

"Those children died from circumcision. Their parents could not afford a casket. They were simply thrown into the forest."

She pointed to a mound surrounded by wild roses and African water lilies. "What's that?" I asked

"Those are the graves of my little ones. One by one, every two years, next to each other, I laid them to rest, giving them into the hands of the Great Ruler of all things."

"Why didn't you stop having children, since you always had twins?"

"My dear Nina, children are a symbol of a man's wealth and honor. I wanted to honor my husband with at least one child. It was my own way of fulfilling my womanhood, giving my husband one decent thing in this life... something no one but God could really give him... something to close the gap between us, to assuage the sadness I felt.

"Did you love him?"

Neka held me tightly to her chest. I knew she was afraid to answer my question. For a moment her grip loosened, and she began running her hand on my head. Her lips trembled as she spoke.

"Yes. It was hard, but I loved him. I had asked God to give me the strength to love him, and with time, it became easier. Before he died, he had tears in his eyes. He apologized to me, and on behalf of his family. He promised that if we were joined in the next world, he would be a different man. Just a simple look and a touch of the hand from him before he died sent utter bliss through my heart. It was a feeling that I never knew that I could feel. It is true...men do not know the joy that comes from a look and a simple touch of the hand. It is a feeling that no kisses, no matter how passionate or freely received, can replace. I was the only one allowed at his bedside before he died. In this unusual way, he was honoring me. And I believe he was truly a changed man."

We heard a rustle, and the breaking of twigs. Neka

pressed her finger to my lips, hushing me to silence. She took my hand. Quietly, we lay low behind an oilbean tree. She whispered, "Twenty-five years ago, I lay hidden behind this tree when my first babies were left in the forest."

We saw Ada and six women place a rolled and tied straw mat in front of the statue. Neka sighed, then whispered, "Ada must have cut too much."

My heart throbbed, and I broke out in a cold sweat. That was the first time I had seen Ada since my circumcision. My body trembled with fear. Ada sat in front of the statue chanting, rocking back and forth, like a deserted child. Her voice rose above the women around her who responded in chorus. Frozen with fear, I thought of the fate of the children in my town, and wondered what would become of them.

Chapter 3

June 1998

The Nigeria Airways flight circled over Port Harcourt. Nina was nervous. Through the hazy morning clouds she could see tiny buildings, tall palm trees, and the imposing silhouette of the Presidential Hotel. She looked at her two associates from Oxford. Their eyes were transfixed on the windows of the airplane. Sister Kristin and Sister Brooke were both wearing habits. Sister Kristin was Nina's age, twenty-five. Sister Brooke was old enough to be their mother, but her mannerisms spoke otherwise, as did her young face. They were sent by Catholic Charities of England to assist in the administration of St. Mary's Hospital in Eze, and would hand it over to the locals in three years.

Nina lifted her palms to her cheeks. They were icy. She turned once more to see Sister Brooke staring down at her. She had a way with feelings. But Nina's concern was for both of them. Though she had left Eze fully fifteen years ago, she knew it would be relatively easy for her to adapt. Sister Brooke and Sister Kristin, however, were entering uncharted waters: no electricity, no running water, unpaved roads, no outhouses for most homes--they used the bush. Eze was one of the more remote parts of Nigeria.

"You must be nervous, Dr. Azu," Sister Brooke said.

Nina was surprised at her formality. Sister Brooke always called her by her first name. "Nonsense. I was born here--I know everyone. It's my people down there."

Sister Brooke didn't notice that Nina was trying to make them feel confident, to count on her knowledge of the people. But, in fact, during the years she had been away from home, many changes had taken place; there were many new things that she would have to learn. Nina's past passed through her mind:

> *I have no one to return home to. I'm the only child. Both my mother and father died while I was in medical school. I couldn't afford to come home for their funerals. The military government reneged on my scholarship, and I was forced to do odd jobs.*

The voice of the pilot came over the intercom. Nina concealed the trouble she felt.

"Ladies and gentlemen, this is your captain speaking. We're making our final approach to the Port Harcourt International Airport. We'll have you on the ground in just a few minutes. I have to advise you that it is unwise to take pictures at this airport. Anyone caught taking pictures goes directly to prison."

Nina looked at Sister Kristin and shrugged her shoulders. Sister Kristin was carrying more film than she would need in a lifetime.

Nina felt a cold chill run through her body as the ground rushed to meet the airplane. Nervously, she took a mirror from her purse and examined her makeup. She applied a fresh coat of lipstick. Sister Kristin and Sister Brooke fell in step behind her as she came down the loading ramp of the airplane. They were instantly greeted by a wave of heat and humidity. Several soldiers armed with kalashnikovs, swaggersticks, and hand grenades stood in formation around the airplane. The number of soldiers were enough to start a medium-sized war. Military vehicles and armored cars flanked the fringes of the airport. Beyond that were miles of forest. Nina patted her, hair which she had pulled back in a bun, and smoothed her skirt against a mild wind.

"You! Over here."

Nina turned to the voice. One of the soldiers had ordered Sister Kristin and Sister Brooke aside.

"Sir, they're my colleagues." Nina began walking towards the soldier. "We're traveling together," she explained.

A swaggerstick suddenly appeared in front of Nina, firmly pressed against her chest. She looked up to see a green beret secured on the soldier's head. He towered over her. His nostrils were unusually large, hairy, and ugly. They flared as he breathed. Nina could smell the musky odor of the soldier's body. Sweat trickled down his neck and disappeared into the crevice between it and his camouflage uniform.

"You must proceed to the arrival hall," he said, giving Nina a non-too gentle push with his swaggerstick.

Nina, herself afraid, stole a furtive look at Sister Brooke and Sister Kristin. They stared at the soldiers nervously, looking lost. Blisters of sweat had formed on their faces. They looked miserable in the 110 degree temperature. Their habits made the heat and humidity doubly oppressive. Nina fared better in her loose blouse, free-flowing skirt, and sandals. With her backpack slung over her shoulders, she took one more look. She wasn't sure what to make of the soldiers.

The small arrival hall was in pandemonium. Against two small customs booths, under a naked light bulb, the soldiers were separating the passengers, and probably robbing them silly. The ceiling fans didn't work, and the ventilation was minimal. Children cried in the oven-like temperature. For a moment, Nina believed that the laws of nature had been suspended at this airport.

Her eyes darted from the arrival hall to the tarmac in search of the sisters. Moments later, completely soaked in sweat, they joined Nina.

"What took them so long with you?"

Sister Brooke gave an unamused smile. "They wanted to make sure we weren't some kind of spies."

"Ha. . . most of the candies we brought for the kids are gone," Sister Kristin interjected, laughing. "Those gentlemen were stuffing their mouths with sweets while they searched our garment bags."

Outside the long corridor, Dr. Patrick Lloyd and his associates from the Ministry of Health awaited Nina's arrival. Dr. Lloyd was dressed in the same fashion Nina had seen in the pictures he had sent to England: rough khaki shorts, cargo jacket, short-brimmed khaki hat, and safari boots. His skin was heavily tanned. His blond hair, much of it bleached by the sun, was curled at his collar. He was shorter and more stout than the men around him. At a glance this English gentleman could be mistaken for a tough Australian frontiersman.

Standing behind him were several of the local elders, looking puzzled. Nina could tell they had never been to an airport in their lives–it could be seen in the way they marveled at the airplanes.

"Welcome to Nigeria," Dr. Lloyd said. "Did you have a good flight?"

"Very much so," Nina replied.

Nina reached out to take his hand, but his hairy blond arm grabbed her wrist, and pulled her against him. They hugged for several moments. Nina sensed the bond and triumph that united them. He had recommended to the government to give her a scholarship to study medicine at Oxford. Dr. Lloyd gestured with a flourish, a gesture that connoted success.

"I'm glad you could make it," Dr. Lloyd said, as he took Sister Brooke and Sister Kristin's hands.

"Glory be to God," Sister Brooke answered.

Music suddenly prepared a welcome song for their arrival. Sister Brooke, despite herself, began clapping and nodding to the rhythm. Somewhat flattered, Nina walked around shaking the hands of the elders, while Sister Kristin took pictures of the locals in defiance of the warnings posted all over the airport.

A few minutes later, the songs trailed off as they were led to a United Nation's bus. When Nina looked back, the elders and their entourage had boarded an old bus, throwing up a cloud of smoke. Still singing, their voices rose above the noise from the engines. Nina recognized their tunes as she sat quietly, consumed by a new spirit of homecoming, her childhood memories racing through her mind.

They arrived at the airport gate. It was the only exit.

Armed soldiers watched as their vehicle approached.

"It is unwise to leave any goods purchased from England exposed," Dr. Lloyd whispered. "They'll find a reason to confiscate them. Of course, the items are never seen again. There are military checkpoints every eight miles."

"Halt!" said the hostile voice of a soldier. He and his underlings surrounded the bus, looking suspiciously inside. But the United Nations logo on the vehicle kept them at bay. After some anxious moments, the soldiers waved them on.

Beyond the gates, under the nose of the soldiers, several young men and women beat on their primitive musical implements. Patrolled by three men armed with bullwhips, their bodies lined with raw welts, they chanted and danced at the command of the men.

The scene was gut-wrenching, their condition all too familiar: filthy clothes, bushy hair, long fingernails. Their faces were bony as if they hadn't eaten in weeks, while the faces of their handlers shone with health.

They approached the bus as it slowed to turn onto the highway.

Bewildered, Sister Brooke looked at Nina. "What's going on out there?"

"They're mad people," Nina said calmly, somewhat embarrassed. Her sense of national pride kicked in for a brief moment. "The country doesn't have sanatoriums. The mad are rounded up by henchmen and beaten into temporary sanity, a treatment that will calm years of schizophrenia. They're patroled to panhandle for their handlers. They've been forgotten by their folks, and the government looks the other way. They're glad the mad are taken off the streets."

44

Sister Brooke opened her purse, pulled out some bills, and reached out the window to offer her money. As one of the handlers approached to receive it, Nina intervened.

"Don't do it. None of those mad men and women will ever see a penny of it." Sensing what Nina had said, the man who had approached gave Nina a vicious look, and stomped his foot in anger. As the car pulled onto the highway, several thoughts went through Nina's mind:

> *I wonder what happened to Uloma, the mad girl who danced at the market. If she were still alive, she would only be five years older than I.*

The one-hour trip from the airport to Eze was silent. The sight of the mad people was one more scene that needed to be absorbed. Sister Brooke and Sister Kristin kept staring beyond the highway at the miles and miles of forest and green foliage. Given the choice at this moment, they would probably have opted to remain in England. What they didn't know was that they had accepted an assignment far more dangerous than they could possibly have imagined.

*　　　*　　　*

The unpaved road was lined with people as the bus, chased by a few children, approached the hospital. Sounds of drums, bells, shekeres, and whistles filled the air--the sounds of the Owu masquerade dance. The locals were dressed in their party outfits: the men wore dashikis, while the women sported rich colorful bubas, headwraps, and long dangling earrings.

Sweaty young boys and girls danced in circles in front of the elders. A small crowd gathered around Nina's car, fascinated by the two white nuns who were going to live among them.

The main hospital building was a row of warehouse-like structures with glass louver windows. The handwritten sign in black and white hung from a cable strung over a wooden plank:

ST. MARY'S HOSPITAL

The thick green lawn around it was uneven, cut by a combination of cutlasses and machetes. Beyond it, in the distance, was the forest of the Haunted Ruins. Ghost-like images of monkeys could be seen as they jumped from bough to bough. Fifty yards away was the cemetery of the new church. Nina's mind was suddenly thrust to the work ahead of her.

She felt a cold hand on her shoulder. "Are you all right, Nina?" Sister Brooke asked. Nina quickly hid her anxiety.

"Yes. . . of course, I'm fine. The heat and humidity, they're just getting to me."

"Have you prepared a speech? You have to say something to these people. They are all looking forward to hearing your voice."

Sister Brooke was right; she didn't know that Nina had prepared a three-page speech months before they left England. But Nina was now uncertain how the locals would receive her. She wanted to pour her heart out to them, to tell them about the thoughts and events that drove her, that haunted her.

Dr. Lloyd was still busy greeting the panel from the local county council and Mr. Ignatius Okolo, the state minister of health, who had just arrived. The dignitaries sat on benches under tarpaulin shades strung up by the officials. Occasionally drinking from their glasses, they were completely engrossed by the masquerade dance being performed at center stage. Several feet in front of them, under the shade of an umbrella, was a small podium that had been prepared as a platform from which the dignitaries would give their speeches.

Dr. Lloyd and Sister Kristin joined Nina. With them was an official dressed in a dashiki.

"This gentleman is with the county council," Dr. Lloyd said. "He will take you on a tour of the living quarters and the hospital. I have to warn you, ladies, there's no running water. The electric generator that is supposed to supply light and pump water from the well broke on the first day, and had to be returned for repairs."

Sister Brooke and Sister Kristin looked at Nina, disquiet in their eyes. Like Nina, they both wanted to use the bathroom. The living quarters were a hundred meters from the main hospital building and the three hospital wards.

They walked silently behind the official. Nina stole quick glances at the hospital wards, military-like dormitories with rows of beds. No privacy for the patients. Nina noticed that Dr. Lloyd looked at them from the corner of his eyes, judging their reactions. He felt uncomfortable with the two nuns. Usually, at such times, he would throw out a few jokes, but not on this occasion.

The official stopped in front of the living quarters and

looked at them. "All right, you know this is not England. Therefore, you must not make comparative judgments. We are grateful the church has helped us to erect this hospital. We're counting on your diligence to make it a success."

He unlocked the first door. It was dark inside, and he quickly began to open the windows through a hole in the mosquito nets. A naked light bulb hung from the ceiling at the center of the livingroom.

"The rooms are the same," he warned. "You may make your choice."

The livingroom had three chairs and a coffee table. No carpets. A black and white television set and a radio stood on a wooden table on the far right corner. Doors on the three corners led to separate bedrooms. In Nina's room was a small steel frame bed with a mosquito net suspended from a crossbeam. A standing fan flanked the window, and next to it was a chair in front of a makeup table.

"I would like to see the bathroom, Nina," Sister Brooke whispered.

"We can manage from here on out," Nina said, looking at Dr. Lloyd and the official. "We'll join you at the main building."

Sister Brooke was the first to dash into the bathroom. Nina could still hear the faint sound of drums from the hospital courtyard.

"Lord help me! Lord help me!" Sister Brooke's frightened voice rose above the drums as she came crashing out of the bathroom. Her face was red with emotion, and her hands trembled.

Nina and Sister Kristin rushed forward. Sister Brooke,

out of breath, clutching her habit in fear. "Something in the toilet! Something in the toilet!"

Nina walked quickly into the bathroom. Buckets of water were lined along one corner for them to flush with. Slowly, she peeked in the toilet. A young lizard had found its way into the bathroom. With a plunger, Nina helped the lizard out. After quieting the sisters, they all took turns cleaning up.

When Nina returned to the courtyard, Dr. Lloyd was waiting for her. He had read the speech she had left with him. "It would be unwise to give your speech as you have prepared it," Dr. Lloyd said, a twinge of concern on his face. "You will only stir a mutiny, given the minds of the elders."

"But we must approach the problem head-on," Nina said. "Those women must be condemned for the atrocities they've committed in this town. The young people are counting on me. I'm the only one they have. Everyone thinks men have power over circumcision, but it's far from the truth. Our women perform the circumcisions. And they're the ones affected by it. If the women do not accept it as a part of their beauty and rite of passage into womanhood, I believe no man in this town would care if his daughter was or was not circumcised."

Dr. Lloyd looked at Nina resignedly.

"This is a war you can only win through grassroot opposition. If you use this hospital as a front, the town won't show up for any treatment. Surely it's better to keep everyone happy at this stage, and avoid rocking the boat."

Nina knew Dr. Lloyd was nervous. Beads of sweat showed on his face. And he was right. It was important that she modify her speech and create new allies.

Nina walked to the small podium. The sounds of drums had faded. Silence had fallen on the audience, except for an occasional cough. The people fanned themselves, trying to keep cool in the torrid temperature.

Nina stood on the podium under the shade of an umbrella. For a moment, her words were caught in her throat. Past experience had not prepared her for the sight before her. In the audience, she spotted familiar faces. Not even the new wrinkles could shield their faces from her knowledge of them and of their atrocities.

Chief Eze sat in a large armchair surrounded by the elders, while Mazi Igwe, who was regarded as the town's chief warrior, watched the events with suspicion. Ada and the six women who had held Nina down on the day of her circumcision stood expectantly in the audience. She felt their bleary eyes staring through her. Hatred and anger shone on their faces. Behind them was Uloma, the mad girl. She clutched a baby in her arms. Only a piece of cloth was draped around her waist. But she was still far more beautiful than the women around her. Looking at her baby, Nina thought, what man could do this to a mad woman?

Nina could hear young children tease Uloma as they walked by. Although Uloma was now a woman, they still called her, "Uloma, the mad girl."

Nina scanned the audience carefully, but she could not find Neka. Was she dead? After all, she had not heard from her since she left Eze for England. Of course, it was hard to receive reliable news from Eze--it had taken one month to learn of her mother's death.

Nina swallowed hard, clearing her throat of a sudden tightness. So many things she wanted to say--so many fingers to point. Her eyes met Doctor Lloyd's. Nervously, she poured a drink from a bottle of spring water on the podium. She lifted the glass to her lips. It wasn't easy. Her hands trembled. Behind her were Sister Brooke, Sister Kristin, and in their new blue uniforms, standing in formation, six African support nurses from the Ministry of Health. Nina turned to the audience once more, adjusted the microphone, and leaned forward.

"Chief Eze, elders, minister of health, dignitaries, ladies and gentlemen. Before I begin, I would like to introduce these two people behind me. Sister Brooke and Sister Kristin, would you please come forward?"

They walked to the podium to stand beside Nina and waved to the audience. "Sister Brooke is the chief adminis-trator for the hospital. Sister Kristin is the head nurse. They have been sent by Catholic Charities of England."

"Ndewe nu!" Sister Brooke's voice echoed through the place. Laughter broke out in the audience as Sister Brooke awkwardly greeted the locals in their dialect. Miraculously, Nina managed a smile, and then pointed at Dr. Lloyd. "Dr. Lloyd doesn't need any introduction. He has lived among you for years."

The audience smiled at Dr. Lloyd.

"It is with great honor and pride that I stand before you. I must also thank you for the great work that you have done in building this hospital. I will forever be indebted to you, and foremost for the support that I received from many of you while in medical school. It will remain a part of me for the rest of my life."

51

"As the new millennium looms, I would like you to join me in the fight to eradicate disease, hunger, and some of the outdated ritual practices that hinder the progress of our children, and endanger lives in our towns. Until recently the birth of twins in this town was a taboo. We lost many children because we failed to listen to our hearts, and acknowledge their right to live, and feel the agony of the mothers who lost their children to the gods of the forest. The only redress we can make to the children who died, and to those living, is to foster our consciences and become aware that the welfare of our children is in our hands."

Female circumcision must also be abolished in this town. We must reject those who etched fear in our minds and have for years taught us that female circumcision has been handed down by the gods of the forest and the spirits of our ancestors. Such beliefs are false, and do not conform with modern times."

Nina looked up from her speech once more. Ada and her entourage had walked off, as had some of the elders. Somehow, they had gotten word of Nina's intentions. But Uloma, the mad girl, watched unwaveringly.

Could she make any sense of my speech? She wouldn't be able to care for her baby. The man who got her pregnant must be found, and punished.

After Nina's speech, Sister Brooke and Sister Kristin joined her as she went about shaking a few hands and making new acquaintances. The African support nurses handed out candies and cans of powdered milk to the children. Nina watched from a distance as the children accepted the gifts.

52

The innocence on the faces of the girls didn't reveal the tumult they had endured from their circumcision, but she knew intuitively that they shared her sad childhood memories. She turned to see the remaining elders leave without acknowledging her. At best, she would convince the young to join her cause, but there was an ominous look on the faces of the elders as they walked away--it was the look the town warriors had when they prepared for war with a rival town. Nina wasn't sure she would survive the dangers ahead.

Chapter 4

July 1998

Nina turned from the window, leaving behind sad thoughts of her childhood and her return to Eze. She was nervous. Sister Kristin could see that in the way Nina paced the small office of the hospital, occasionally returning to the same window and lifting the lace curtain to look at the flood-swept road. It was the African monsoon, and the flood waters cut gullies along the unpaved roads. Nina turned to look at Sister Brooke. "Dr. Lloyd isn't coming," Nina said. A certain tightness in Nina's voice revealed her anxiety.

Sister Brooke did not look up from her desk. "He will come," she answered calmly as she flipped through a newspaper. But her voice lacked its usual force. She, too, could not concentrate. She looked up from her newspaper, and her eyes darted at the pictures on the wall. Assorted pictures of animals Dr. Lloyd had taken while saving endangered elephants from poachers in Tanzania hung on the wall.

Nina looked at Sister Brooke. "Do you think the army. . .? It isn't like in England. There he always came at the snap of a finger."

Sister Brooke gave a faint smile. "We're now in Nigeria,

things are different."

Nina walked to the back window. In the next ward, she looked at the still body of the young girl on a gurney with a white sheet draped over it. Blood seeped slowly through the white sheet and onto the floor.

It could have easily been me years ago.

In the distance, through the mist that covered the glass louver, she stared at the forest of the Haunted Ruins. Mist rose from the waterfall beyond the hills. The acacia tree that grew over Chichi's grave must be swaying in the wind and the torrential downpours. She walked to the door of the morgue, and saw that the blood from the young girl had finally stopped collecting into a pool on the floor beneath the gurney.

Several hours had passed, the rain had stopped, except for a gentle drizzle that fell quietly on the hospital courtyard. Then suddenly a brilliant blue sky appeared, the sun casting orange rays in the trees. It was always like this, the rain and the sun, mixed and in competition. Now a mild wind blew against the trees. Nina watched as the villagers passed by on foot and on bicycles. She heard the hum of a vehicle approaching. Dr. Lloyd's jeep slowly undulated through the gullies the recent downpours had created.

"Dr. Lloyd is here," Nina announced. The two sisters rose from their seats and walked to the door to meet him. They watched the jeep come to a stop. Dr. Lloyd got out, and walked briskly to meet them.

He took their hands firmly. "I came as soon as I heard. Is she in the morgue?"

"Yes," Nina answered. "I have sent for her parents to

remove her body."

Nina led Dr. Lloyd into the morgue. She put on a pair of surgical gloves and pulled off the sheet that covered the girl's body. Sister Brooke and Sister Kristin stood in formation.

"This is a five-year-old," Nina said. "Judging from the color of her eyes and her lips, you can tell she had hemorrhaged extensively before she was brought here. In fact, she was practically dead upon arrival. I could do nothing for her."

Nina held the girls legs apart. "This is the most radical form of circumcision. It used to be unique to Egypt, but it has found its way here through the Muslims. As you can see, this is a total infibulation. The clitoris, labia majora, and labia minora have been removed. The two parts of the vulva have been sewn together to ensure chastity. The two small orifices that you see have been left for the passage of urine, and menstrual blood when she comes of age."

Nina looked at Dr. Lloyd, then at the two nuns. "Basic circumcision cuts the clitoral hood, this is called *sunna*. Normally, this does not impair a woman's sex life, but does impose some psychological trauma. In some cases, they perform *excision*, in which the whole clitoris and the surrounding tissue are removed."

Nina gently pulled the sheet back over the girl's body. She saw the tears in the nuns' eyes. Quiet fell in the morgue as Sister Brooke began to recite the Rosary.

Moments later, a small van arrived to remove the girl's body. As they watched the van drive off, a movement under the acacia tree caught Nina's eyes. A woman was standing under the shade of the tree. Her baby was crying. They were both wet from the drizzle. Nina walked to investigate. The figure grew familiar as she got closer.

"Good evening, Nina." Uloma was standing in front of Nina. When her baby saw Nina she stopped crying.

She knew my name. Could this be a moment
of temporary sanity?

They embraced affectionately. The locals who saw them were taken aback. They could not understand Nina's liking for a mad woman. Nina's heart pounded as Uloma handed over her baby.

This is one girl that won't be circumcised in
this town!

A small crowd gathered around them. Nina, fearing the locals and what her actions might spark, took Uloma and her baby into the hospital. She knew word would spread that a mad woman had entered the new hospital. The mad were outcasts of the town.

"I never stopped thinking about you," Nina said. "How old is your baby?"

"She's two."

"She's a very beautiful girl," a voice sounded behind them. Dr. Lloyd had entered the room.

Nina noticed Uloma's nervousness when Sister Brooke and Sister Kristin joined them.

"Everything is fine," Nina said, placing her hand reassuringly on Uloma's shoulder. "Who's the father?"

Uloma shrugged her shoulders. But she met Nina's gaze. "He raped me. No one would listen." Tears fell down her cheeks.

Nina pulled out a chair from her desk.

"Here, have a seat," she said, helping Uloma into the

chair. "You do know this man, don't you?"

Uloma lowered her head slightly. "I'm afraid. He would kill us both if he finds out I told you. He has said it so many times. He always comes on Friday nights after drinking at the bars at the fish market."

The small office grew quiet as Uloma began rocking back and forth like a lost child--chanting and singing:

Our beautiful maid roams
the forests in the moonlight,
dancing to the songs of moon and stars,
while the darkness sings of her beauty.
Animals of the night join in chorus,
gods of the forest turn from her sorrow,
leaving her in the hands of an evil man. . .

Sister Brooke handed Uloma a glass of water. A chill went through Nina's heart as she felt the evil forces that were destroying the town. She looked through the window and saw, in the distance, the forest of Haunted Ruins. She saw as in a mirage the image of Chichi and her mother floating in the orange sky. Gripped with fear, she sought to connect with her past:

What will I find when I return to the forest?
Chichi's grave holds painful memories of my
own childhood, but if I bring back the past, I
will summon the courage to guide me through
the future.

Slowly, Nina turned to Uloma. "I will not let this man get away with what he did to you, if it is the last thing I do in this town."

"We must find her a shelter," Sister Brooke said.

"She can live in one of the maids' quarters," Sister Kristin suggested.

"If you do that, none of the locals will ever come to this hospital for treatment," Dr. Lloyd said.

Nina studied Uloma for a moment. "Dr. Lloyd is right. I will see that you get help outside the hospital."

Nina knew Neka would be the one who could help Uloma. If she could find her, Neka would know the best way to help without sparking an outcry from the people. Nina was sad to see Uloma leave, knowing that she and her daughter would return defenseless to their little hut at the market square.

Nina's thoughts focused on finding her friend Neka. *Was she still alive?* Nina yearned for their reunion. Several times she had sent for her, but her aide couldn't find her. Neka was the only person she could trust.

Chapter 5

The next morning, under the faint light of dawn, Nina left the hospital. She concealed her face with a dark silk scarf and avoided the locals as she walked over the unpaved road and on into the forest that led to the marketplace. A light dew fell, mixing with the smell of wild flowers and the musky odors of the forest, filling the morning air with a poignant odor like the beginning of *harmattan*, the dust-laden African wind. As she walked in the sand, Nina studied the paws and tracks of wild animals that had crossed during the night. Croaks from crested franklins, the hoot of owls, and the barks from monkeys in the tree canopies brought back childhood memories. These were the memories of Eze she liked to relive while in England. This was her true homecoming.

Nina came to the market square. She approached nervously, making sure no one at the market noticed her. She looked at her watch. It was five o'clock in the morning. It was still early, and the large number of hawkers who clamored their wares hadn't arrived yet. But within the next few hours, the stalls would be filled with local merchants. Far on the fringes of the market, flame rose quietly into the sky. As Nina got closer, she saw Uloma lying on a raffia mat; she and her baby huddled against an open fire. Nina could not help but wonder what would become of them.

If Neka and I help them too publicly, we might turn the entire town against us. It might be better to leave them alone, at least for a while, but make sure they have adequate nourishment and medical care.

Uloma was cooking in the open flame in front of her hut. Nina picked up Uloma's baby.and she began crying, but Uloma took no notice of Nina. She just continued to add wood to the burning fire while the baby quieted down.

"Good morning, Uloma." Nina waited a few moments for a reply, but none was forthcoming. She sensed that this was a prelude to an outburst of schizophrenia. Uloma would remain quiet for hours, sometimes even days before explosive episodes. She remembered when she was a child, during an episode, Uloma would sometimes walk around nude in the market square, or engage in acrobatic dances.

Nina looked inside the hut. It was constructed of palm frond, and an earthen floor. A raffia mat was on one end, occupying the entire length of the hut. On Nina's right were empty food cans and assorted types of rubbish and paraphernalia which Uloma had collected around the market. Pieces of cloth hung on the palm frond, Uloma's only clothing.

Nina nervously placed a hand on Uloma's shoulder, afraid of Uloma's reaction. Uloma could lash out at her in a crazed rage, and perhaps no one would come to Nina's aid. She was far stronger than Nina.

"What are you cooking?" Nina asked, peering inside the pot. The small pot was filled with yam porridge. Nina saw the translucent palm oil floating on the surface. It reminded her of her childhood, when her mother made the same dish for breakfast. But then she wondered whether Uloma could keep track of time, of meals.

Is she really going to feed her daughter this early?

"When will you come to visit me again?" Nina asked. Uloma still didn't respond. Afraid to ask further questions, Nina kissed Uloma's baby, and gently placed her back on the raffia mat.

Nina walked briskly past the market so no one would see her.

Could it be true that the gods of the forest and voodoo have made Uloma go mad?

Several years back, she had convinced herself that black magic and voodoo were only a myth. But now, she wasn't too sure. Subconsciously, she had feared Ada for a long time. The more her fears grew, the more evident her voodoo powers became. She wondered if Ada could successfully put a voodoo spell on her. *Will I become mad like Uloma? Imagine living under such conditions.* Not even her years in England could completely erase her fears of voodoo, and the impact Ada had on everyone's mind.

Her thoughts still unanswered, she began running, afraid and uncertain whether she would meet an evil end.

*   *   *

Not realizing how far she had run, having left the market square a long way behind, she came upon a road that narrowed to a path in the forest. Through the faint light of dawn, the iroko tree grew larger as Nina approached. She saw peregrine falcons perched on the high branches. As a child, she had loved to watch the acrobatic flight of the falcons as they tried to catch other birds in midflight.

Nina took her usual position at the base of the large tree and waited. She studied her surroundings. She could hear noises from the other birds, crickets, and the cockcrows in the distance. Suddenly, an uneasy quiet fell on the forest surrounding her.

> *Have the animals become frozen because of my presence? Is a large predator lurking around the tree, causing the animals to freeze? Am I in some kind of danger?*

Nina's thoughts ran rampant, and her heart beat in her throat. A slight rustle in the small path startled her. As she looked in that direction, she felt a sudden peace, and her heart filled with joy. She rose to her feet, arms outstretched.

It was Neka, walking with a limp. She supported herself with a small cane.

> *She must be at least fifty. She is still beautiful, not a single wrinkle has marked her face.*

"Princess!" Neka took Nina in her arms, and squeezed her against her chest. This was what Nina's mother always called her. Nina's sobs filled the forest. She wished to be reunited with her mother both in mind and spirit. Through Neka, she could revisit her mother's soul, feel her sense of being, and immerse herself in her mother's love.

"I'm so glad to see you," Nina said. "No one was able to bring me to you. I was afraid I wasn't going to see you again."

Nina couldn't tell whether her tears were of joy, or of

mourning for her parents.

They embraced for what seemed like minutes. Neka continued to run her fingers across Nina's head. "It's all right, Princess. They cannot break our spirit.I heard of your return, but I could not make the trip to the hospital to see you. None of the young men would bring me. You see, my knee has been damaged by the disease they call arthritis. Not even the local herbs can help me.

"You are such a beautiful girl, Princess," Neka continued, and held both palms against Nina's cheeks as she spoke. She wiped the tears from Nina's face, and once more pulled Nina against her breast. Neka too had tears in her eyes.

They sat at the base of the tree. Neka offered Nina several udala fruits, as she always had when Nina was a child.

Filled with emotion, Nina accepted the fruits with trembling hands. "You don't know how much this means to me to sit here with you. I never thought this day would come."

"You've always warmed my heart, Princess," Neka said. Her voice was resonant with feeling. "I too never thought I would be reunited with you. My only regret is that you weren't home soon enough to save your mother. If it hadn't been for the civil unrest, she would have lived. There would have been a hospital open to care for her."

Nina grew more sad. Her lips fluttered. She knew the story of her mother's death would be difficult, but she wanted to hear it and thereby find peace in her mind.

Slowly, Nina looked at Neka. "Will it be difficult to tell me what happened?" Nina's voice sounded like a child's. She wasn't sure she was really ready for this.

"It will be difficult, Princess, but it is my belief that the only way that I can reunite you with your mother is to tell you her story. Even under incredible duress, she never lost her love for you." Neka took Nina's hand.

"It was about ten o'clock in the morning," Neka said, and shifted from the uncomfortable position in which she sat. "The sun was bright, but it felt good against the skin. A gentle wind rustled the forest. Both the sun and the wind were mild, the skies tranquil. It was a day in which a beautiful maid would have loved to sun herself on her raffia mat. Your mother and I looked at the blue sky. Though the sun shone brightly, we could still see the moon. The moon was so large that we felt we could reach out and touch it. We looked at ourselves, and smiled at the weather.

"We were going to have fun. After gathering fruits from the farm, we planned to bathe at the local stream. As we walked, I heard a voice. I could have sworn it was your father calling your mother, but he was on a business trip at Aba, fifty-five miles away. Your mother, too, heard the voice. We looked at each other. She hesitated for several moments. She always believed in telepathy, and now had a premonition something had happened to your father. I was also afraid. We wanted to go back home, but we changed our minds, blaming our uneasiness on Ada and her voodoo.

"About twenty minutes later I heard your mother scream. She began calling my name. I ran to her. As I got close, I heard her praying. She had stepped on soft earth, and it had caved in around her foot. When she lifted her leg from the small hole, her left ankle was bleeding. Her cut had an unusual contour, and a stirring within told me that she had been bitten by a snake. I began yelling for help, but we were three miles into the forest."

"Did you tie something around her ankle to prevent the venom from spreading through her body?" Nina was standing, on her feet, agitated.

"Yes, I did. But it didn't help. As I began to lead her home, she lost her sight. It was a very powerful venom. She had a problem walking, and was beginning to drool and foam from the mouth. Her breath was labored, and her pulse irregular."

Nina took a few steps, and sat back down next to Neka. *The venom was gradually shutting down her nervous system.* Nina stared straight in front of her.

Neka nodded, as if Nina were conversing with her. But she knew Nina was reaching into her own inner mind and thoughts.

"We rested for a few minutes, and I urged her to go on. You see, I thought if I could get her to continue walking, we might reach her home in time to get help. But thankfully, we met a hunting party. Four young men carried her the rest of the way."

Neka looked at Nina. "If only any of the hospitals had an anti-venom. You see, it was during the wake of military takeover, and the height of civil unrest. All the hospitals in the distant towns were poorly managed. Night and day, we could hear the protesters in the distance. Our only doctor had joined the revolt, and the few white doctors had gone back to England and America."

Nina stared at Neka, who was immobilized with guilt and shock over her mother's agonizing death.

"What about the local medicine man? You know the

one... the voodoo doctor."

Neka shook Nina's hand. "Once we got home, we sent for him. When he arrived and saw your mother's symptoms, he threw his hands up in the air in defeat. He immediately knew that she had been bitten by a black mamba. Many people would have died within the hour, but since she was still alive, I had hope." Neka covered her face in both hands, then continued:

"When we arrived at her house, she could no longer speak coherently. Her leg had swollen to three times its size, and her wound had changed color. When morning came, she was in still more pain. She wanted to be held by your father, but he hadn't returned from his business trip. The next day she wanted to be placed in your room. Somehow she sensed she was not going to live, and it was her way of being reunited with you."

For a few moment, the sadness in Neka's eyes made her seem much older than her age. Nina placed her arm gently around Neka's shoulder.

"*Oga adi nma*," Nina said, and repeated in English, "All shall be well."

"Her wound was gradually being eaten by the venom," Neka went on. "The third day, mixed with blood, clumps of tissue began to ooze from her wound. By the next morning, so much tissue had fallen out that her ankle bone was visible. She had not slept for a moment, and her eyes had rolled back in her head. When your father returned, he was distraught. He immediately rounded up some young men, and they took her on a bicycle carriage to a hospital that had opened twenty-five miles away. Everyone was hopeful. We thought the hospital would save her.

"When the doctor cleaned her wound, he removed five snake fangs which had lodged in her ankle tissue. You see, when one is bitten by a mamba, often the fangs break off in the skin. This is why the snake is feared by everyone. The venom left in the fangs break down the tissue. The doctor told us he had done everything he could to save her, but it was too late. A few hours later, your mother fell into a coma.

"Throughout the night, your father stood by her bedside. He never lost hope. When morning came, we saw her move, and again we were happy. Your father began calling her all the sweet names he had for her. In a brief moment in her delirium, she uttered a word as if in response to your father. It brought tears to my eyes to see the love between them. Then, just a moment later, she stopped breathing. The nurses and doctors tried to revive her, but she didn't respond. She lay peacefully, her faced beaded in sweat.

"It took three strong men to remove your father from her side. Two days later, she was buried among her townspeople. Since your mother was the first daughter of her parents, she could not be buried in a foreign land. She had to be buried in the town where she was born. Your father wanted so much to bury her among his people, but our town's chief wouldn't allow him to disregard our custom.

"For months, your father withdrew from everyone. His behavior became erratic. He would walk for miles talking furiously to himself, for you see, he was slowly dying of grief. Two years later he fell ill. One morning, he didn't come out of his house. When two young men knocked down his door they found his body lying peacefully. He must have been dead for a few hours."

Nina was deep in thought while Neka looked at her. Then Neka placed her arm around Nina's shoulders. The sun shone lightly and was soothing against the skin, and a mild wind blew across their faces. Leaves disturbed by the wind showered down from the trees.

"It is a beautiful day," Neka said, trying to stir Nina out of her painful thoughts. "You are a very strong girl. Your father and mother loved you so much. They are now in the hands of the Great Ruler of all things."

Nina heard the breaking of twigs in the forest, then voices. She looked at Neka for a brief moment, then in the direction of the noise. Ada and the six women who had circumcised her were walking through the forest in their direction. Nina and Neka stood up as they approached.

"I'm giving you and your friends one week to find your way back to England," Ada stormed. "You are no longer welcome in this town. You are a disgrace to us all, to our culture and our people. You have brought nothing but shame by telling us that our way of life is inferior to the ways of foreigners. There are some of us who want to see you dead, but I'm giving you the opportunity to leave with your life."

Neka stood between Ada and Nina. "Where is your conscience, Ada?" Neka said. "This is neither the place nor the time to engage in this malicious talk. The poor girl has just come home from miles away and is mourning her parents. Now, you want her dead, too?"

Ada took two steps. A violent slap tore across Neka's

face, knocking her to the ground. "You barren whore! You couldn't even have the right sort of children. You can't even walk properly. You are no longer one of us. Don't forget you were sold to this town. Now you think you have the right to speak?" Nina pounced on Ada, knocking her down and pinning her to the ground, her hands clamped around Ada's neck, choking her. She felt Ada's hand groping behind her neck, and felt a slight scratch from a fingernail. Then several blows and kicks smashed into Nina's sides and back. She was being attacked by the six women. Nina freed Ada, and one by one, she fought off the six older women.

"She's crazy!" one of the women yelled. "She will pay for what she did to Ada. She will pay with her life!"

The women fled from the scene, and Nina ran to Neka. "Are you all right?" Nina asked, helping Neka to her feet.

"Yes, Princess. But I think you are in trouble. Now they want you dead. Those women will stop at nothing till they get their way."

"I'm going to be fine. My cause is just, and my mind is clear. No one should be afraid of Ada and her voodoo. If anything, it is she who should pay for the lives of the children she has killed in this town through circumcision."

But inwardly, Nina felt strange. It was as if she were falling ill. She felt floaty, and her spirit seemed to have been taken from her. She felt a certain urgency to get back to the hospital.

"You don't understand, Princess. She will turn the whole town against you."

"I'll be all right," Nina said finally, and kissed Neka on the chin. They hugged tightly. But Nina's nerves were unsettled by her body's spastic twitching.

"I brought some medicine from England that will help your knee," Nina said nervously. "Please have someone bring you to the hospital for treatment."

Nina then bade Neka goodbye. As they departed, waving, both knew what was in the other's mind. They were afraid of Ada, but wouldn't acknowledge it. Nina was consumed by her thoughts as she walked through the forest. Neka's warning was hard and clear in her mind. She could not control the trembling in her hands. She thought about one of the women's threat: You will pay with your life.

*   *   *

The sun now shone with intensity, but the wind was still mild. Nina felt unbearably hot. Her anxiety did not help. She took off her scarf. Suddenly, her strength seemed to be draining. Her legs felt weak, and her breathing was labored. She sat down slowly on the path. She felt a stream of heat running down her back and touched it with her finger. It was blood. She remembered Ada's hand reaching across her back. One of Ada's fingernails was unusually long and pointed like an eagle claw. Then, Nina remembered as a child a story her mother had once told her:

> *The sorceress would tape a small eagle claw on her finger. In the groove of the claw was a tiny sponge that held a juice made from poison. She killed her enemies with it. A single scratch and a light squeeze and the poison is injected into the victim's body. The*

anesthetic effect of the poison prevents its victim from knowing he has been scratched. Our ancestors used the poison for hunting big game. They rubbed the poison on the tip of their arrows. Once an animal was shot with the arrow, the poison was delivered into the bloodstream. Not even an elephant or giraffe was safe. Smaller animals died within minutes, larger ones in hours."

Nina forced herself to resume walking, realizing the urgency of receiving an antidote. She was thirsty, and licked her tongue trying to induce saliva, but only managed to rub against her own dry skin. Then, as her nerves began to shut down from the poison, she started to tremble. Her jaw muscles became weak, and she found it hard to close her mouth. Fever began to wrack her body as the poison stirred up antibodies in her blood. The time it took her to reach the hospital seemed interminable.

"My God, what's wrong with you?" Sister Brooke was the first to see Nina.

"I've been pierced with a poison dart," Nina said, and collapsed into the nun's arms.

"Help!" Sister Brooke yelled.

Dr. Lloyd and Sister Kristin ran into the room.

"She's been poisoned by a dart."

Quickly, they placed Nina on a stretcher and wheeled her into the small emergency room. The six African nurses got in each other's way as they set up an IV, and the small room was soon a hive of chaotic activity. Nina's cheeks were pale and sunken, her eyes enormous, her lips on fire.

She had a burning pain, like a red hot iron through her breast. Her eyes rolled back in her head and sweat poured from her body.

"We don't have an antidote!" Dr. Lloyd exclaimed, dropping his head, then looking up despairingly at Sister Brooke and Sister Kristin. They knew Nina had only a few hours before she would go into shock, then the coma would set in from which she might never recover.

"The Federal Ministry of Health!" Dr. Lloyd exclaimed. "They must have an antidote."

"That's at least two hours from here," Sister Kristin said, "and if they don't have it?"

But Dr. Lloyd ran out, jumped into his jeep, and raced down the rough road.

Sister Brooke and Sister Kristin said a quick prayer, then Sister Kristin began placing a series of cold water packs on Nina's head to reduce her temperature, while Sister Brooke set up a second IV.

An hour passed, Nina's head burned with fire and she was in terrible pain. She tossed and turned as if the death agony had begun. Not once did Sister Kristin leave her side. Every so often Nina's body shook with the fever. She became delirious and rambled on about her mother and father, about wanting to go home to the hills where she was born. The sweat from her body began to seep through the sheets. She was being dehydrated methodically by the poison and was so weak that you could hardly tell she was breathing. Now and then, she seemed to improve, and she would talk--the type of fanciful talk people engaged in before they die. She talked about how the world would be a better place if all people treated each other with love, and how all would be reunited in the next world in brotherhood. She went on about how she had never married and had children of her own, but dreamed of chasing her children through the fields and collecting wild roses from the forest.

Both sisters had tears in their eyes. They were afraid Nina wasn't going to make it. Sister Brooke looked at her watch. Dr. Lloyd ought to be back in ten minutes or so with the antidote. But she feared Nina would lose the functions of her major organs before then. She had heard tales of the kidneys going, then the liver, and finally the heart. The hum of approaching vehicles broke through her thoughts and she looked up. An ambulance and two police cars were speeding toward the hospital with Dr. Lloyd close behind.

Sister Brooke met Dr. Lloyd at the door. "Did you get it?"

"Yes. How is she holding up?"

"Not too well," Sister Kristin said as Dr. Lloyd and the officials from the Federal Ministry of Health walked into the emergency room.

Dr. Lloyd quickly injected the antidote into the IV. "The antidote could be toxic if delivered directly into the bloodstream," he said.

The room was quiet. All eyes were fixed on Nina as they waited for the antidote to take effect. Dr. Lloyd took one of the police officers aside.

"The evil person who did this must be brought to justice," Dr. Lloyd said.

The police officer smiled but shook his head. "We came to provide escort so you could get to the hospital as quickly as possible, not to investigate any crime. You and I know this poison cannot be traced in the body. The government hasn't even established a method of forensic inquiry. Until someone catches this person in the very act, everyone in this town is at the culprit's mercy. We have dealt with several other cases in remote towns, but the perpetrators are protected by the local chiefs. Everyone fears their magical powers."

"She's opened her eyes and her breathing is more even!" Sister Brooke exclaimed happily.

Dr. Lloyd rushed back into the room, this time with a smile on his face. Nina's normal color was seeping back into her face. Dr. Lloyd looked at his watch. Within the next fifteen minutes the poison would have left Nina's system completely. He placed a hand on her forehead. The fever, too, had broken.

Several minutes passed. "I have a massive headache," Nina complained, and sat up in bed. Her face was tired, her body drenched in sweat.

"Stand and walk around a bit," Dr. Lloyd said. Sister Brooke and Sister Kristin reached out to help.

"I'm fine," Nina said, and held out both hands to stop them. "Really, I'm fine." She rose and took several unstable steps, but soon steadied.

"I should be fine by tomorrow," she said firmly. But she knew how close she had come to death and of the dangers ahead.

I'm the only one who can stop this woman.

Chapter 6

August 1998

One month later, Nina stood under a mango tree with the principal of St. Augustine High School. They waited for the students to assemble in the chapel, which also served as an auditorium. The building was like a shack by Western standards. It was cheaply built of brick, and a corrugated iron roof, but surrounding it were wild roses of assorted colors, African water lilies, croutons, and perennials.The manicured lawns were maintained by the students, using only machetes as tools. The building was old, the ambiance reminded Nina of old monasteries in England. Bees and butterflies sucked on the nectar of the flowers. Nina paused for a moment to reflect on the beauty of the school grounds and what the students had done with them.

This was Nina's first outing since her encounter with Ada. She thought she would recover within days, but the effects of the poison left her weak and groggy for weeks.

"Good afternoon, students. My name is Dr. Nina Azu. I would like to introduce you to my colleagues, Dr. Lloyd, Sister Brooke, and Sister Kristin. They are visiting from England. We also have with us an official from the Federal Ministry of Health, Mr. Ignatius Okolo."

A slight murmur rose from the audience at the presence of the three white dignitaries. Some of the students smiled, while others stared curiously. Nina pointed to the official, the cabinet secretary. He was overweight, dressed in a perfectly tailored Parisian suit, with enormous arms and skin like the color of black olives. He looked out of place, his suit looked more expensive than the old building.

"How many of you know about female circumcision?" Nina asked, as she walked in front of the high school students. She looked at the boys and girls fixedly. Only fifty hands were in the air.

But there must be five hundred of them.

They were the senior students from eight different high schools in the state. Their teachers watched from one corner.

More out of the girls are too shy to respond.

"I can see that only a few hands went up. Well, this is why we're here today. I'm sure most of the girls have gone through this torturous experience. I assure you that when you leave here today, you all will have learned something about female circumcision and the consequences to our girls from this outdated practice. Do not feel shy or intimidated to participate in this seminar. We will all become more educated about this subject so that we can solve this problem.

"How many of you know why girls are circumcised?" This time more hands went up. The students were gaining confidence. One particular student drew Nina's attention. He raised his hand higher than the others.

"Why don't you stand up and tell us?" Nina said, pointing to the student.

"Well, several adults have said that it is a hygienic and

aesthetic practice."

Nina waited until the student took his seat. "That's one of the reasons that has been argued," said Nina. "Can someone else give us another reason?" Another student stood up. This time, the student walked in front of the audience with an air of confidence. He looked at Nina, then nodded at Sister Brooke and Sister Kristin.

"It is a critical rite of passage into female adulthood. A woman must be circumcised or no man will marry her. I believe that we have no right to question the customs set forth by our great-grandfathers. It's really a shame that we are doing this in front of these foreigners who know nothing about our culture. What's good for you and your foreign friends may not be good for us. So this discussion is not necessary."

Nina was taken aback by the young man's self-assurance, bordering on effrontery. She looked at the health official. His face beamed with pleasure.

"You're right in a way," Nina said. "The issue you've raised is plausible."

She looked into the audience. "We need to hear from some of the girls too."

But another boy walked to the front of the stage. Nina was amazed to see the girls sit placidly, not uttering a word.

"Female circumcision is necessary for a woman," the boy began. "It reduces her sexual desires, thereby ensuring premarital chastity and later, conjugal fidelity. An unmarried woman's mobility is also reduced,.she doesn't go looking for partners in distant towns. And therefore, she doesn't marry far from her family. She also doesn't become a harlot."

At this, a young girl walked briskly to the front and stood on a small pedestal in front of the audience. "It's really appalling to sit here and listen to these young men speak so eloquently about issues they know nothing about. Everyone in my family was circumcised. I lost a sister due to complications from the operation. And now I've heard the arguments my fellow students have made so arrogantly. The fact that some of the participants seem ignorant of the dangers of circumcision is almost as disheartening as the practice itself.

"It is difficult for me to stand here and tell you how my family has suffered from this butchery, but I believe that a human being with a conscience will not allow his daughter to go through this ritual. I watched my younger sister die at the age of four, she bled to death. I was at her side throughout her agony."

Tears welled in the girl's eyes. "It wasn't until after her death that we found out she was a hemophiliac. Soon afterward, my mother committed suicide. She thought she was doing the right thing bringing her daughter up by following local custom. But she felt responsible for my sister's death. I have lost the two most important people in the whole world. Only my father and I remain."

The pain in the girl's eyes almost moved Nina to tears herself, but she knew she had to remain in control.

"These dignitaries are here because our town needs help," the girl continued. Her lips quivered as she spoke. "They are the ones without a biased opinion. The practice of circumcision is so deeply rooted in our culture that if we ask our elders to fight against it, it's like asking 'the fox to guard the hen.' Therefore, we should stand up and give these foreign dignitaries a round of applause for having come thousands of miles to help us."

Nina hugged the student as applause filled the auditorium. She then turned and smiled at Sister Kristin and Sister Brooke as they stood up to be honored by the students. Sister Brooke raised her hand for quiet. Nina nodded and waited for the noise to subside.

"Ndewenu," Sister Brooke said, greeting the students in their local dialect. Nina smiled. It was the only word Sister Brooke had picked up since her arrival, and she still said it awkwardly.

"I'd like to thank you, students and teachers, for allowing us to be a part of this discussion. Like Nina said, we are here to learn about ourselves and the effects of female circumcision. Growing up in England as a child, I never had to worry about most of the issues that confront you today. It breaks my heart to see that most of your parents are so far removed from the realities of these problems.

"You have a rich culture, which fascinated me as a child. Being here with you today is a fulfillment of my childhood dreams. Every one of you should be afforded the opportunity to travel to distant lands, make new friends and acquaintances. And you should not be burdened with some of the outdated practices that do not conform to modern times. It is my belief that you, the new generation, should not have to make the difficult decision of whether to have your child circumcised. As for us, if we can save one child through you, we will together make the world a better place. Your children will be indebted to you because you have protected them.

"You--you are the ones to educate your parents on this issue, you are the ones to carry the torch of victory. The world will look at you with joy, knowing that you have given your daughters the right every child deserves--to grow up as God-given children, untainted by a death-dealing practice. When you leave here today, I encourage you to read an article from the newspaper. We have given copies to your teachers. You will learn how the world looks with horror at this practice, and you will read about the opinions of students from around the world.

"Thank you for giving me the opportunity to speak in front of you, and may God bless you all."

A wave of applause trailed Sister Brooke as she walked back to her seat. The small auditorium grew silent. The students seemed engaged in thought.

Nina walked back to the small pedestal. "How many of you know of the different types of circumcision?" she asked. She waited, but no hands were raised.

"Did you know there are three major types of circumcision?" The auditorium was still quiet. The students looked at each other in surprise. They weren't aware of the different types. This practice has been so secretive that not even the girls discussed it among themselves. Often, they weren't aware of its consequences until they reached sexual maturity.

"The first type of circumcision is referred to as *excision*," Nina explained. "The clitoral glans or the whole clitoris is removed. The second form and the most radical is *infibulation*, where, along with the clitoris, the labia majora and minora are removed, and the two parts of the vulva are then sewn together. Two tiny orifices are left for the passage of urine, and for menstrual blood when a girl comes of age. This form of surgery is practiced mostly in Egypt. On the girl's wedding night, a boiled egg is inserted into the girl's vagina through the small orifice. If she doesn't bleed, then it is believed that she had engaged in premarital sex and may be rejected by her new husband. In some cases, if the egg fails to penetrate, the orifice is widened with a scalpel, razor or dagger. The last form of circumcision is *sunna*. This constitutes cutting the clitoral hood or the prepuce. It is believed that it does not impair a woman's sexual life, but it often presents psychological trauma. These practices are performed by both Moslems and Christians; but no teachings in the Koran or the Bible suggest the practice of female circumcision.

"Several arguments have been made by some of the students; for example, that female circumcision reduces a woman's sexual desires, thereby ensuring premarital chastity and conjugal fidelity. This is false. The removal of the clitoris may reduce sensitivity, but it cannot affect desire, which impacts psychologically on every woman. Moreover, such practice robs women of their civil rights, of self-determination. Every woman should have the right to enjoy sex. It is an integral part of the life experience and both husband and wife should enjoy it. Society has no right to control this God-given experience.

"The other argument that has been made is that female circumcision is more hygienic, and more aesthetic, and that it constitutes a woman's rite of passage into adulthood. Yet, it is a proven fact that Western women today are healthier than our women. Most women here suffer from chronic infections attributed to circumcision."

Sam Asinugo

Nina looked through the window and saw that a small crowd had gathered outside the building. A man came to the door accompanied by four other men. They marched up to the pedestal.

"The chief has ordered that this meeting be adjourned. He also has ordered that you meet with him and the elders at his quarters immediately," the man said.

Nina looked at the cabinet secretary. "We have permission from both the state and the local government to conduct this meeting," she said.

The man threw up his hand. "You may have gotten permission from every government official, but I cannot disobey the local chiefs. It is neither my place, nor do I have the authority."

Nina knew that the man had only come to make a show for the government, as if they cared about ending female circumcision. They had no intention of educating the public. Gradually, the teachers walked out, one after the other. And the cabinet secretary followed. He gave Nina a wry smile as he walked through the door.

Nina watched as the crowd grew outside. She could see the worried look on the faces of both sisters. They seemed to be waiting for a cue from Nina. Dr. Lloyd meanwhile was speaking with one of the chief's men, trying to get him to quiet the crowd. When Nina turned around moments later, most of the male students had walked out, but the majority of the girls remained.

"It doesn't look good for you and your friends," the chief's man said in broken English. "The whole town is angry about your teachings, and for bringing these foreigners to teach our

84

girls to be harlots. You must go directly to the chief and explain yourself."

Nina looked at the man. "Now?"

"Yes. Now."

"I would like at least to have some government officials present. We can't simply allow you to drag us to the chief. You know what your orders may engender--the crowd outside is very unstable."

One of the students came between them. "Don't be afraid of the crowd. We will all go with you to meet with the chief. Every one of us heard your speech, and your teachings, and we want to assure you that you have our support."

Nina was the first to leave the building, with the students trailing behind her. She was greeted with the loud tom-tom of the village talking drum, the voice of the gods. It never sounded for nothing. It was a frightful sound, one she had dreaded as a child. It only sounded when something extraordinary occurred or a danger threatened the town. Everyone, no matter who, was required to drop all activity and report to the chief's quarters at once. It was a call for the speedy assembly of the community, and instructions were then issued. The last time Nina heard the drum was when she was ten years old, during the burial of the eldest chief. The scary burial ceremony was still etched in her mind.

Nina was now frightened. The entire community was milling towards the chief's house. Noise spread through the dusty roads, as both young and old rushed towards the chief's quarters. No one wanted to be late. Nina could hear people ask each other the reason for their assembly, only to receive a frustrated shrug of the shoulder. But one thing was clear, the students weren't speaking to the locals. They walked steadfastly behind Nina, Sister Brooke, and Sister Kristin, as if providing a shield between them and the throng.

The chief's quarters were located on a hill, surrounded by high walls, and fresh vegetation, which turned yellow during the dry season and brown during harmattan. Large banana leaves grew over the walls, flanked by towering coconut trees. When seen from a distance, the compound gave the appearance of an anthill surrounded by large mushrooms and short vegetation. It was the largest compound in the whole town, it had to be. The chief was married to fifteen wives. This meant a house for each wife, which she shared with her children by him. The chief's main house was strategically located in the middle of the little houses. In the very front was an *ibari*, a tent-like porch, where he entertained guests and held important meetings for the town.

When Nina arrived, the compound was filled to choking. Men on one side, women and children on the other. Nina's stomach churned as her eyes met Ada's. The sorceress took her place among the elders, and pretended not to notice Nina. The titled elders were seated in a semicircle at the center, isolated by a small shrine. Their eyelids were colored traditionally with chalk, which was supposed to ward off evil spirits. Four statues of gods stood in strategic positions separated by a wrinkled dirty white cloth. A stout man recited the usual litany to the gods of the forest, thunder, and lightning, as he waited for the chief to make his entrance. Nina eyed Sister Brooke and Sister Kristin. She knew this was opposed to Christian teaching. Given the chance, Nina knew Sister

Brooke would spray the multitude with gallons of holy water.

A sudden silence fell over the people as the chief made his entrance. It was as if the sun were making its long-awaited appearance after a large storm. A slight wind blew across, then, spewing odor from the direction of the shrine, the decaying matter from the sacrifices that had been made to the gods--chicken, eggs, and goat intestines.

Chief Eze had had the town named after him. It was a tradition of his family for generations. A tall, large man, with prematurely greying hair, he had a dignified walk, much like the Pope walking through the Basilica of St. Peter in front of a multitude. He had been the strongest wrestler in his younger years, and he was still handsome; most women found him attractive. His father, too, had held several titles for valor, which made the chief's family the envy of other towns. His aides walked behind him, one carrying an *agada* chair on which the chief would sit.

Chief Eze motioned for his aide to set his *agada* down. He took his seat in the middle of the elders. He was then presented with a cola nut. He broke it, said the usual litany of prayers to the gods of the forest, then passed it to the elders. But he whispered words loudly enough so that the elders could hear him, but not the crowd. Nina felt that they were talking about her.

Slowly, the chief rose to his feet, surveyed the crowd, and cleared his throat. From the corner of her eyes, Nina could tell that the chief had taken a good look at her. "My fellow citizens of Eze, I have called you here because something unusual, something terrible has happened in our town. But before I begin, I ask that the women and children leave. Only the men and our visitors must stay." The chief pointed at Nina, Sister Brooke, and Sister Kristin.

A disgruntled murmur rose among the crowd, mostly from the women. The chief gestured. Suddenly there was silence. "I know how you feel, but I promise that your husbands will inform you of the outcome of our meeting. Right now, I must ask that you leave."

Gradually, the women and children dispersed, leaving the men and Ada. Her privileges were immeasurable. She was ranked ahead of most of the men.

"Why are you still here, children?" the chief asked, looking puzzledly at the students in their khaki and white uniforms.

Nina stepped forward, and respectfully bowed. "They are participants in the state-approved education program against female circumcision. They came with me to speak to you."

One of the students came forward. She too bowed to the chief. She spoke quietly, but unafraid, unintimidated by the elders. "Dr. Azu is right, Chief Eze. In fact, we can't leave without Dr. Azu and her colleagues. We believe that she brings a breath of fresh air to our youth. After all, we sent her to England to learn the new ways things are done. Everywhere you look, changes are taking place. New hospitals are being built, more women are going to school and have taken jobs as doctors, teachers, and clerks. Dr. Azu is the only medical doctor from this town, and we have deep respect for her accomplishments."

Chief Eze looked baffled. No one in his life had ever

disobeyed his orders. But his anger was subdued. "Well, children, if you insist." He looked at the elders with his hawk-like eyes, then at Nina, and the nuns.

"Our women and children are our most important asset," he said sternly. "This teaching against female circumcision has to stop. We have lost too many girls to city life, they have become harlots. They have no intention of getting married, of having a normal adulthood and blessing their husbands with children."

Chief Eze pointed at Nina as he spoke. Nina stared at him. *There is something godlike about this man. Could it be that I still have fear of him as I did when I was a child? After all, he was the one who met with the oracle of the hills, the most feared god of the forest.*

Chief Eze paused for a brief moment, disturbed by the creak of the double doors of the gate as they opened. The chief stiffened. Uloma, the mad girl, walked into the compound clutching her baby. Chief Eze looked nervously at the elders. A mad woman showing up at their meeting wasn't a good sign. Uloma walked with an air of indifference past the elders. Her baby, recognizing Nina, struggled out of her mother's arms and leaned forward with her arms outstretched. She wanted Nina to carry her. Chief Eze could not believe his eyes; even the students were taken aback. But the students relaxed when Uloma's baby began gurgling happily to Nina, like any baby. The silence in the compound was thick enough to cut with a knife. The elders were transfixed, looking at Nina holding Uloma's baby.

"It hurts me to see that you have chosen a different

path," Chief Eze continued, looking at Nina. "That child you are holding and the mother belong to the oracle of the hills. You have no right to hold her. Her mother is a bridge between us and the gods of the forest. Her family was given to the oracle to appease the evil spirits that were going to invade our town."

"Hand the child over, Nina," Ada said, walking over to Nina.

"Why?" Nina asked. "So you can circumcise her? You have taken the lives of many children in this town. Now you want her to be another victim of your practice? Don't even get close to me. Everyone knows what you did to me."

"I don't know what you are implying, but the child doesn't belong to you."

"Oh, no you don't! I'm the last person in this town who will sit around and see a child die at your hands. The gods of the forest must have known from the beginning. Isn't it why they never blessed you with your own? Only an evil childless woman like you would kill children through circumcision. You have broken the hearts of many mothers, and no one has ever dared challenge you. But look around us, look at you, and the people of this town. In only a moment, your world will come crashing down. It has happened in distant towns, and our town is next."

The hum of an approaching vehicle interrupted Nina. Dr. Lloyd and two armed police officers got down from his jeep.

Chief Eze looked at the titled elders, then at Nina. "All this show of force does not intimidate us. The state supports our will and self-determination."

90

"Since I was a child, I have always had great respect for you, chief," Nina said. "But so many changes are taking place before our eyes. It wasn't too long ago that twins were left to die in the forest of the Haunted Ruins. We lost too many children. Most of them would have grown to be healthy adults, and would have had children of their own. Many mothers were left heartbroken. Today, having twins is a blessing from the gods. Does this mean that the gods of the forest got tired of seeing innocent newborn babies killed by our town? If this is correct, then they must also be tired of seeing our children killed by the woman that sits before you. Ada has killed more children in this town than all diseases combined. In fact, only a few weeks ago she poisoned me with her nail. You cannot let her evil ways go unpunished."

An uproar went through the audience. They had not expected Nina's boldness. None had ever stood up against the chief.

"You are a harlot," Ada said. "And you should die like one. You have brought nothing but shame to our town. You are no longer a part of us. Everywhere you look, our girls are running around with men, having premarital sex, something your parents would never have allowed. Your mother and father would be aghast to see what you are doing. You are teaching our children the ways of the devil."

"Quiet!" Chief Eze shouted. "I would like the two of you to stay outside the walls of the compound." He pointed at the two police officers. The two uniformed men looked at each other, then slowly followed his orders. Chief Eze was smarter that Nina had thought. The chief didn't want Ada to make any incriminating statements in front of the police.

"I hereby order you to stop your teachings on female circumcision. You and your friends must leave this town at once."

"I do not wish to disobey you, chief," Nina said respectfully. "But you are not being fair. Whatever happened to the kind chief my mother always told me about--the one who gave back lands wrongfully seized by his father? Was it only a ploy to win the chieftaincy from your brother? This is my town. I was born here, just like every single one of you. I will not be driven out by Ada nor anyone who supports her. She has also made an attempt on my life, and I'm not going to be quiet about that either."

Nina turned to Uloma. "What town allows a mad woman to get pregnant? Is it not the law of this town that anyone who gets a mad woman pregnant should be put to death? Did not our great-grandfathers believe that getting a mad woman pregnant brings a horrible curse on our town? We have turned a blind eye to these activities due to the corruption in our town. We can no longer sit around and let mad women be raped by our town's men. She wasn't made pregnant by the gods of the forest. If it is the last thing I ever do, I will find the man who got her pregnant and expose him."

It was as if Nina were speaking in tongues. She was grappling with something, something neither Sister Brooke nor Sister Kristin could put their finger on. A long silence fell. Everyone seemed to be at a loss for words. The chief had been taken by surprise.

"Come, students, let's get out of here," Nina said finally. A small crowd was still gathered outside, most of them children.

They ran as Nina and the nuns walked out.

Within minutes, they reached the school. Nina handed Uloma her baby, while the students surrounded her.

"I'm forever indebted to you for your support, " Nina told the students. "You have shown the courage of kings, without regard to the reactions of your parents when you get to your homes. I assure you that you did the right thing. Female circumcision is not a good tradition, but a grave injustice, and a death sentence to many children. As a child, I lost a very dear friend, her name was Chichi. You never met Chichi, but she was the sweetest girl you would ever know. Chichi died in front of me. She never lost her courage, and loved her parents to the very end. When you get home today, I want you to talk to your parents, convince them that this practice is not good for our girls."

Nina paused for a moment, and looked into their eyes. She felt a special affinity for the students.

> *Could it be the way they valiantly stood up against the chief or the life I never had as a child? Could it be that they are going home to their parents, and I don't have anyone to go home to?*

"Feel free to visit me any time at the hospital," Nina said finally. Nina and the two nuns watched as the students scattered on their way to their various homes. Uloma followed, going towards the market square.

Dr. Lloyd pulled into the school grounds. "You want to hop in?"

Nina was the last to enter the car. She was watching Uloma.

"What were the police for?" Nina asked. "You know the chief has the police in his pocket. Didn't you see how they walked out quietly at his command?"

"Yes, but the crowd was at least taken aback by their presence. You know how irritable that crowd was. When you have that many young adults, a riot is almost inevitable. Knowing how corrupt the chief is, he might easily have incited the crowd to attack.

"Look, I think it's getting dangerous around here. We must consult the Federal Ministry of Health and ask for some protection. You can't live in the hospital quarters without it. And I hate to tell you, but Sister Brooke and Sister Kristin's superior has ordered them to work at the hospital during the day, but to stay at the parsonage at Owerri at night. I tell you, it's far too dangerous for anyone to sleep at the hospital. Anything can happen. Worse still, I've been reassigned to a mission in Honduras. I must leave Nigeria in two days."

Nina looked at Dr. Lloyd in horror. "I can't believe this is happening. You've been reassigned, Sister Brooke and Sister Kristin can't stay at the hospital quarters, I've been told nothing. . . Who will attend to the children when they are brought here at night?" Nina asked, as if begging Dr. Lloyd to change his mind. "They always circumcise the girls at night or in the early morning hours. This means that the girls who hemorrhage will die if I'm not there. There's no way I'll agree. I'm here to save their lives. Even if only a single child is saved, I will know that I gave my best."

The jeep stopped in the hospital courtyard. Dr. Lloyd came down from the car, and took Nina's hand. He led her through the garden, away from the others' earshot. "I'm saddened by my departure because I've enjoyed working with you. It is moments like this that cause me to question the integrity of our superiors, but we must trust their decisions. You've committed your life to saving the lives of your town's children, but one must think of self-preservation. Anger looms in this town against your teachings on female circumcision. From this moment on, I would like you to record the events around you. Do not leave any detail unnoted. It is the ones that you ignore that will get you killed."

He handed Nina a tiny camera. "You do remember my trips years ago to Tanzania's Sarangheti game reserve to save endangered elephants from poachers, don't you? Well...this is a night camera. It is the latest of its kind. Be sure to take pictures of anyone that comes within twenty meters of the hospital at night. This way your superiors will have evidence to show the government, should something happen."

He continued leading Nina through the garden. Nina pondered what Dr. Lloyd had just said about her danger as they walked. She knew that she had drawn a battle line with Chief Eze. One month ago when she lay near death from Ada's poison, she had Sister Brooke and Sister Kristin to help her. Now she felt alone and afraid. How would she be able to defend herself against the chief? Her fear made a tight knot inside her. She feared she might die somewhere cold and dark.

Chapter 7

September 1998

Nina walked in the foothills of the forest. A feel of solitude pervaded the place. It was in the foaming waters from the falls, and, beneath, the murky shade of the lime walks and the ravines, full of mist and stillness, laden with the smell of wild roses and ripe *ubene* fruits. The forest seemed untouched from the years to the ordinary eye, but a denizen could notice the small changes that had taken place. On the far side of the valley, a dirt road had been built, and the locals passed by in groups. The distant hum of a passing vehicle could be heard, something Nina had never noticed as a child.

Nina took a different path. It was rocky. She climbed guardedly through the ledges, until she joined the familiar path. Beneath it, several small streams raced each other, as they fed into a large gorge. The water broke the silence, gurgling noisily through the gorge into the lake basin.

Nina paused. The voice of a woman rose clearly above the torrents. Nina could not tell where it was coming from. She listened to the voice. At first, it sang an odd tune, slow and melancholy, then rose to an outburst of sound. She followed the sound,walking quietly through the narrow green glades between the *ubene* plants. The air was filled with the sweet aroma of the fruits amidst the blossoms of southern grasses. A chill went through Nina's body, and her heart pounded against her ribs as she ran the rest of the way down to the valley until she saw the wide expanse of the lake in front of her. It was as broad as the Thames at London, she thought irrelevantly.

A woman sat on a fallen log that reached halfway into the lake, her feet submerged in the water. She slowly treaded water as she sang. She was too far for Nina to identify, but she remembered every note of the song. It was an old Anglican hymn:

> *Rock of ages, cleft for me,*
> *Let me hide myself in thee.*
> *Let the water and the blood*
> *From thy riven side which flowed*
> *Be of sin the double cure,*
> *Cleanse me from its guilt and power.*
> *Rock of ages cleft for me,*
> *Let me hide myself in thee...*

Nina's eyes gleamed with tears as she took several steps. It was not only the suddenness of seeing the woman, it was the beauty of the place, intoxicating like the magic fragrance that sometimes wafts from the letter of a loved one. The place was filled with serenity and opulent beauty. An occasional wind whimpered against the tree branches, and the birds were quiet, as if relishing the scented air. To call it aesthetic would be an injustice, and to think it normal would be to evoke the curse of the gods.

It was Neka. Neka could not see Nina from where she sat. With bad legs, only a courageous woman would make such a journey through the hills of this land. Her song rose and fell with the sound of the water. Nina's approach was masked by the gurgling stream as it flowed through the crevice in the rocks and fed into the lake. Then a rock, loosened by Nina's footstep, dropped from a ledge and tumbled several feet, falling into the lake. The noise from the splash echoed through the hills.

Suddenly, the song ceased. Nina couldn't tell if Neka had detected her presence. "Good evening, Mama," Nina said in a subdued voice. Nina felt the bond of blood between them, as she had had with her own mother.

Neka lifted her wrapper to her face to wipe away the tears. She cleared her throat, then paused before she spoke. "It's so beautiful out here."

Nina knew Neka had been taken by surprise "I didn't expect to see you here," Nina said.

"Me neither, Princess. Do you know what day this is?"

"It's September 12, 1998." Nina said.

"You are right, Princess. It is the anniversary of the day my first twins were born. It's their birthday. They can't be alone on their birthday." Neka turned and looked at Nina. "You agree with me, don't you?" Nina sat on the log beside Neka. They hugged tightly and Nina felt a tightness in her throat. "It's strange. It is Chichi's birthday too, and I've come to be with her."

"I'm glad you remembered. You are the only one she has."

They rose to their feet and carefully stepped from the log onto the rocky ground. Nina looked at the blue sky and saw two herons fly over the lake. She marveled at the beauty of this great liquid field. The crystal-clear lake was as serene and gentle as havens were intended to be. Somehow, nature had found a resting place for innocent children far from the cruelty of a culture that had so mistreated them.

*Could it be that nature has a way of redress-
ing injustice to the young?*

Nina helped Neka over the higher ground. Nina sensed that Neka was growing older and weaker. And then she heard Neka talking to herself in a deep dramatic monologue, but Nina could not make out the words. Neka threw her head back and forth as she spoke. An instant later, both her speech and head movements ceased. It was then that Nina looked deeply into her eyes. Neka's beautiful eyes were sad, and slightly vacant. The youthful texture of her skin was fading, and her spontaneous smile had disappeared altogether, replaced by a blank stare and withdrawal. Her hair was unkept, and her clothes looked as if they had been worn for days. Not once did she engage in their usual talk of the fun they shared when Nina was a child. Nina had the sinking feeling that Neka, like Uloma, had gone mad. Nina was engulfed with sadness and loss ... and fear. Neka was her only ally against Ada.

Moments later, Nina came face to face with the life-sized statue she had feared since childhood. Her hands trembled when she saw yards of grave sites, as if it were a marble orchard. Some with crosses, and some without. Several toys littered the graves. A makeshift monument had been built over Chichi's grave.

*Some parents must have begun to bury their
children the normal way, instead of simply*

*placing them in the forest. It's amazing how
time changes people.*

Nina looked at Neka. "I thought Chichi's parents were dead. Or did someone else erect this monument?"

"I did. It's the only decent thing I could do for her, knowing how much you loved her." Neka left Nina's side and walked over to Chichi's grave. Again, she began to talk furiously to herself, her head bobbing back and forth as she picked the weeds that had grown around the grave. Nina's cheeks paled, for she detected the early warning signs of Neka's illness. Losing her children, and having been ridiculed by the whole town, she had finally lost her sense of being. Nina was afraid she could never help Neka.

Nina turned her attention to a nearby hovel made from palm frond, close to the graves of Neka's children.

"What's that?"

Neka gave Nina a blank stare, but didn't answer. Nina walked to the site. "Have you been living here?" Nina peered into the hovel. There was fire wood, a cooking pot, a lantern, and a small bucket.

"I can't let you do this, Mama. It's not right. You can't let them win like this. You've come too far to give up. They took your children from you, and now they want your soul. You can't let them do it! You're going home with me." Nina quickly began to dismantle the hovel. Within minutes all the palm frond were on the ground. Neka never uttered a word except to talk furiously to herself. Then she walked over to one of her children's graves. Again, she began to pluck the weeds from the grave, cursing the gods of the forest for allowing them to grow so fast.

Nina walked over and took Neka by the arm, but then she heard some twigs breaking. She looked up. Sister Brooke and Sister Kristin were coming down the valley towards them. Nina and Neka watched as the two women approached.

"You didn't leave with Dr. Lloyd?" Nina asked.

"Don't be silly, Nina," Sister Brooke said. "We came here for the same reason you did. We've spoken to our superior and convinced her that our duty is with you." Then noting Neka's condition, Sister Kristin said, "Come, let's get Neka to the hospital. I believe we can help."

Nina led Neka up the hill, but as they walked, she feared that Sister Kristin might be mistaken.

*　　　*　　　*

Nina opened her window at five o'clock the next morning. Her room was filled with the scent of flowers from the modest garden outside. But a storm cloud was forming, and seemed to be coming toward her. Drifts of white petals from the flowers, disturbed by the wind, rose up around her window, lining the base of the mosquito net. She had a great view of the forest of Haunted Ruins and the three hills that surrounded it: to the east lay Udi with its rocky outcrop which looked like a hat on a bald spot; to the west Mbaa, clad with its greens and tall palm trees, like an old witch with plaited hair that pointed recklessly in all directions; while to the north Umueze, larger than the others, stood dignified with the crystal clear lake at its crater. Despite the storm clouds, the air was pure and fresh, the forest full of color, and the animals sang to greet the new day.

Nina turned from her window at the sound of footsteps. "Neka is gone!" Sister Brooke said.

There was utter disbelief in Nina's eyes. "What do you mean she's gone?" Nina retorted.

"The nurses say they never saw her leave. Could it be that she went back to the hills?" Sister Brooke's suggestion lay in the air as Nina shot past her.

"She must have gone to the market!" Nina yelled as she ran down the dirt road. "Today is Afor. It is the day everyone goes to trade their goods at the market. But Neka is not well enough to be there."

Nina's heart throbbed as she half-ran towards the market square. Nearing it, she slowed to a walk. She was in the midst of a noisy throng, most of them women and children carrying large baskets of goods to sell. It was the usual sight, which reminded Nina of her childhood when she and her mother would travel to the market. As she approached the square, she could see smoke rising in the air, most of it from the local butchers and the hawkers who operated roadside restaurants. The aroma from spiced game meat, akara, and fried ripe plantain filled the air. For a moment, Nina was lost in sweet reminiscences as if her mother were buying her akara, and ripe plantain, which she would dip in a sauce of peppered palm oil.

Nina took her usual path around the market square, by now so familiar that she almost failed to notice what was happening. Then she saw Mazi Igwe waving a machete as he ran past her towards a gathering crowd. This was not a good sign. Nina knew Mazi Igwe's reputation as a fierce warrior. More people ran past her, and soon the small crowd grew into a mob. It was the usual mob that gathered when a thief was caught at the market. Nina peered through the crowd. At the center, sat a shirtless frail old woman.

It was Neka! Nina stiffened, her heart beat loudly in her throat. She was weak from fear. She tried to listen to discover what had happened, but in her mind, she already knew. Neka was bleeding from the nose and mouth, and blood flowed from welts across her breasts and back. It was the usual beating given to a thief when caught stealing in the market square.

"She's not a thief, for Christ sake!" Nina screamed as she fought her way through the crowd. She fell on her knees and held Neka against her chest, tears falling down her cheeks. Shielding Neka with her body, she looked at the crowd. "Please allow me to take her back to the hospital. I promise you she is not a thief."

"Get up!" a man yelled, and prodded Nina with his foot.

Nina looked up. It was Mazi Igwe, the man who had ran past her earlier, waving a machete.

"Please don't do this," Nina pleaded. "I'm the doctor of the new hospital."

The man looked at the crowd. "Oooh...she's the one who has been teaching our children the evil ways. Now you want to have us believe that this woman doesn't know right from wrong?" This time, he kicked Nina hard, knocking her and Neka to the ground. The crowd began throwing sand at them, chanting, "Kill the thief and the harlot."

Nina continued to shield Neka with her body as more blows landed. Then a bullwhip rose and fell sharply on

Nina's back. The lash sent a searing heat through her, and her body shuddered. Nina turned to the man with fear-filled eyes, her lips trembling. "I have done nothing to deserve this!" she cried. "I'm one of your daughters. Why are you doing this to me?" She looked around to search for someone--anyone who would listen.

At that moment, she saw Ada standing in the crowd. Ada had a sneer on her face and gave Nina a knowing look. More people had gathered and the crowd was growing more angry.

Suddenly, two gun shots rang out. The whole place grew silent. Then, a stampede broke out as the crowd scattered and ran in all directions.

Nina and Neka gradually sat up. Sister Brooke, Sister Kristin, and two armed police officers were standing where the crowd once was. "Are you both all right?" one of the officers asked.

Nina turned and looked at the two policemen and shook her head. Her lips quivering as she fought for control. "I need to get her to the hospital," Nina said. The pain from the bullwhip engulfed her and her body ached from the kicks and blows of the crowd. She turned to Neka.

"Get up, Mama. We have to get you to the hospital." She tried to get Neka to her feet, but then realized Neka couldn't move. One of her legs had been broken to keep her from running away. Nina went down on her knees and examined Neka's leg. Not once did Neka cry out. Her lack of reality shielded her from her pain.

Sister Brooke worked quickly, securing Neka's leg, while Sister Kristin stabilized her to transport her to the hospital.

"And you, are you all right, Nina?" Sister Brooke asked. "I'm so sorry," she said, with pity in her eyes.

Nina nodded. "I can't forgive them for what they did to me. I have done nothing to deserve this type of treatment."

"They aren't aware of the iniquity of their actions," Sister Kristin said comfortingly. "They're driven by unthinking emotions, egged on by their leaders. You've done nothing wrong, Nina."

They carried Neka into an old minivan, as the crowd slowly began to return.

"That woman stole from the market and must be handed over to the chief," Mazi Igwe said. "The punishment for stealing is death. You have no business interfering with the locals. You should go back to the city where you belong. This will not be the end of the matter."

The police officers waved on the minivan. Nina looked on as the police blocked the people, but objects thrown from the crowd land on the roof of the minivan until the car disappeared into the turn. Silence fell as the vehicle undulated from pothole to pothole. Blood seeped through Nina's bandages and ran down her body. She looked through the window at the dark clouds. The sun had still not made an appearance. It had been two hours since she left the hospital, but it seemed like days. Rain began clattering urgently over the roof of the old minivan. Soon a strong wind was rocking the trees, and blowing the rain inside the van through a broken window. They tried to shield Neka from the rain, but she was already soaked.

It was a ten-minute drive to the hospital. On arrival they

placed Neka on a gurney and wheeled her into the ward closest to the doctor's living quarters. Nina gave her a sedative shot, and within minutes Neka was asleep. The nurses then tended to her wounds, and within the next hour they had set a cast around Neka's broken leg. Nina took a final look at her as Neka's leg was being suspended in the air to improve her circulation.

"All right Nina, you're next," Sister Kristin said. Nina followed Sister Kristin to the private ward. She lay on the bed and stared at the ceiling while Sister Kristin treated her wounds. A sad thought from her childhood filled her mind. She remembered lying on a raffia mat in Ada's hut on the morning of her circumcision--her fears, her sense of desertion, her emotional breakdown. She wished somehow she could be reconnected with both Chichi and her mother. She wanted someone to hold her and reassure her that her works would not come to a meaningless end. As the sting of the medicine on her wounds went through her body, the threats issued by Mazi Igwe raced through her mind: *This will not be the end of the matter.* Nina knew these threats all too well. She wondered if she and Neka would survive the anger that lurked in the town of Eze.

Chapter 8

Later that evening, a knock sounded at Nina's door. It was a moment she inwardly feared would come.

"You must release her to the chief," a voice demanded defiantly on the other side.

Nina stood by the door, contemplating her next action. The police had gone, and there was no one to intervene if things went badly. She counted to ten, then with trembling hands she gently turned the doorhandle. She swallowed hard as she and Mazi Igwe came face to face. It was he who had waved a machete at the market square and flogged her with a bullwhip. Nina looked at the crowd of twenty, then down the dirt road. Her heart pounded as she saw more people heading towards the hospital. Sister Brooke and Sister Kristin jumped into the jeep which Dr. Lloyd had left behind, but just as quickly someone reached into the car and took the key from the ignition. "No police this time," the man said. For a moment, Sister Brooke struggled with the man, but she was no match. Nina looked on helplessly, and feared what would happen next.

It will only be a moment, and then they will come rushing into the hospital to search for Neka.

Nina went to the door. "She's still under my care," she

said. "I can't release her to the chief. Only a few hours ago she had her leg broken and received a beating in your hands, and now you are asking me to release her to the same fate?"

"She has to answer to the chief for what she stole in the market. You are aware that the punishment is death?"

"How can you put a mentally ill woman to death? Our town took her twins, and sacrificed them to the gods of the forest. You took her dignity, her self worth, and now that you've driven her insane, you want her dead? Where is your conscience?"

"Are you going to ignore the orders of the chief and keep this woman in the hospital?"

"Neka can't defend herself. If the chief values justice, then he must allow her to recover sufficiently to stand trial in front of the elders. As it is, she can't even walk. So please tell the chief that I promise to surrender her to the elders in three weeks."

"No!" a voice sounded in the crowd. "Why must we listen to you?" a man said, as he fought his way to the front of the crowd. "We want her now!" The man turned to the crowd. "My fellow people of Eze, are we cowards? When have we ever allowed a harlot to dictate to us what to do? This woman has entered our schools, and taught our children the ways of the devil. And now she has disobeyed us all by not releasing this woman to the chief."

A murmur ran through the crowd, and they jostled toward the double doors. Some began chanting: "Kill the thief and the harlot...Kill the thief and the harlot..."

"Quiet!" Mazi Igwe exclaimed. The crowd grew still.

"You all know me. I'm Mazi Igwe. The doctor is right. We, the people of Eze, have always been a principled people. We must do what is right. I share your thoughts and beliefs. However, we must give this woman a chance to defend herself. If she dies at our hands wrongfully without a trial, her blood could be a curse on our town. And this curse could be carried down through generations. Therefore, we must take the doctor's words to the chief."

Relief flooded through Nina's heart; she wasn't sure what she felt, and whether to thank Mazi Igwe. After all, he was the one who had led the crowd at the market square. She and Mazi Igwe stared at each other for a long moment, without exchanging words. Nina then turned and walked into the hospital while the crowd dispersed. She met Sister Brooke and Sister Kristin in the doorway; for a moment they remained silent. Each knew what was in the other's mind. It could be too late to save Neka's life.

*   *   *

Two weeks later, Nina drove the jeep to the edge of the forest of the Haunted Ruins. It was six o'clock in the evening. She parked the car and walked half a mile up the hill onto a rocky outcrop. She made a clearing, pulled her cape around her, and sat on a stone. She gazed into the distance. It was the only side of the lake that did not hug the forest. The torrents that fed the lake roared after the previous night's storm. Three fishermen in dugout canoes slung their nets over the water, fishing for tilapia and tiger fish, the staples sold at the fish market on the east bank of the lake. The sunset cast

111

orange shadows over the lake and trees, and a gibbous moon was high in the southeast sky. On a distant tree perched a king fisher. Nina watched as the bird dove into the water, emerging with a fish. She wondered whether the fishermen had the same luck.

An hour had gone by, perhaps more, while Nina sat lost in thoughts about the events that were happening around her. Looking to the other side, she had a clear view of the town. The fish market was closing as the town prepared for the night. It was now dark, and although the moon had come out, it was clouding over. A mist lay over the lake, and the faint lanterns from the town glimmered over it. Then she was startled by voices--a young woman's and a child's. The voices took turns, rising in pitch. Nina sat up, when a man's voice drowned those of the woman's and the child's. The man laughed raucously, the laugh of a drunk in a late night bar.

Turning from the lake, Nina started down the steep and narrow pathway through the ravines. She made her way with difficulty down the steep slopes, until she saw the outline of a man at the foot of the hill. He had a woman pinned to the ground as he raped her, her baby whimpering nearby. A chill went through Nina's heart. Slowly and silently she descended the rocks, her heart beating fearfully. Within minutes, she reached a ledge close to the ground. As she swung herself over a branch, the tree shook slightly under her weight. Disturbed by her movements, rocks landed close to the woman. Startled by the noise, the man froze. He looked around searchingly, but could see no one. The noise that Nina made had been all but drowned by the cries of the woman's child. Nina's heart pounded against her chest as the man continued his assault amidst the painful cries of the woman. Nina didn't dare interfere, despite the horror of the scene.

Within minutes, it was over. Nina watched the man leave. She couldn't recognize him, but he seemed to be in his mid-thirties. She walked cautiously towards the woman, fearing the man would hear her and would return. First, she picked up the baby, then walked to the woman.

"You'll be all right, Uloma," Nina said soothingly.

Uloma was startled by Nina's voice, she gasped for breath. Nina hugged her. "I saw the whole thing. You must help me catch this man."

Uloma continued to shudder, as she took her baby from Nina. Then, suddenly Uloma picked up a small bag with her other hand, and walked towards the market square, leaving Nina without a word. Several thoughts went through Nina's mind:

What was she doing here, anyway? Could she have come to fish at the lake like most women? But that couldn't be. None of the baskets used to catch the shell fish were around.

The cloud lifted away from the moon and it became almost as bright as day. Nina looked at the edge of the lake and saw two boats. It didn't make sense to her. She had never seen Uloma paddle a boat. She left puzzled and climbed up the hill to the other side of the lake to reach her car. Her mind raced, as she climbed with a sure foot. She had more questions than she had answers. Moments later, she reached her car. Inside, she held onto the cold steering wheel and stared into the distance, pondering how Uloma had been trapped by the man.

> *He couldn't have carried her from the market square to the lake. He would have risked discovery by the locals and the punishment would have been death.*

She saw in the distance several fishermen dock their boats on the east bank of the lake. Could it be that the man who assaulted Uloma was a fisherman too? Then, all of a sudden, it all became clear to her. It was a Friday night. The fishermen sold their catch to merchants on Friday to be resold at the local markets Saturday morning. But you could only get to the fish market by boat. Nina was now sure that Uloma must have paddled a boat to the other side of the lake and that the bag she carried held the fish she had brought from the fish market.

> *She wasn't allowed to use the same dock as the town's women, and so had to paddle half a mile to reach an isolated dock. The man must have paddled after her from the fish market and ambushed her as she docked her boat.*

Nina drove down the road. She looked at her watch; it was nine-thirty. She didn't pass a single soul. She pulled into the hospital. She knew it would be risky, but she had to catch the man who had assaulted Uloma. She would have to wait till next Friday. Could he be the father of her baby? Thoughts raced through Nina's mind.

A movement under an acacia tree caught Nina's eyes.

Neka was walking with crutches around the hospital grounds, with Sister Brooke and Sister Kristin following closely. Neka's leg had healed faster than Nina had thought it would.

"She's making remarkable progress," Sister Brooke said, but her voice lacked its usual force. Nina nodded her head, knowing what was on Sister Brooke's mind. In one week they would have to surrender Neka to the chief. She wasn't sure Neka would receive a fair trial. Not even the government could stop the locals if they decided to take her life.

Neka turned to Nina abruptly. She seemed to know what was on Nina's mind. "I'll be fine," Neka said ruefully. "I didn't mean to put you through all of this." Her tone was contrite and she seemed anxious. Nina couldn't believe her ears. This was the only conversation Neka had had with anyone since she had been attacked at the market square. She was responding to treatment, and her mental illness seemed to be at least in temporary remission.

"Then you know what happened at the market square?" Nina asked.

Neka shook her head. "Only after I was brought to the hospital. The nurses told me."

"You do know about the trial then, don't you?"

"Yes, Princess. And I'm not afraid."

A warmth went through Nina's heart when she heard Neka call her "Princess." It seemed like old times, but she was aware of the complexities of mental illness, and its temporary swings. But hiding her forebodings, Nina reached out and hugged Neka tightly. At least for the time being, she felt she had regained a lost friend.

"You're aware of the consequences of this trial?" Nina asked. "You may lose your life."

Neka smiled pensively. "My children need me. It's always been my prayer that, somehow, we will be joined in the next world. What is there to live for? I have neither a husband to share my sorrows, nor a mother or father. Everyone has departed, but me."

Silence fell in the hospital courtyard. When Nina looked behind her moments later, she saw that the nuns had gone. They had apparently left her to be alone with Neka.

"You shouldn't speak in that manner, Mama," Nina said. "There are a lot of other women who have lost their children in this town. They all look up to you. Many died of a broken heart. But through it all you remained the champion of those who lived. If you give up hope, all will be lost. Oh, Mama, I've been so hurt by the events of the past few weeks. I know that it's not your fault, but sometimes I wonder what happened to the woman who always gave me my inspiration? The highlight of my day was when you would bring me udala fruits. Now I may lose you to Ada and the chief. Knowing the resentment in Ada's heart, she may incite the chief to deny you a fair hearing."

Neka froze for what seemed like minutes. She gazed into the distance, staring at the full moon. Nina could see the sorrow in Neka's eyes. A mild wind blew across their faces. Disturbed by the wind, dew that had collected on the acacia had begun to drip down to the garden.

"I'm so sorry, Princess," Neka said, with tear-filled eyes. "Sometimes life seems too hard for me to bear. But we certainly can't let them win. We could simply run, but what then would be the fate of our women and children? No, we'll fight them with all the strength left in our bodies." Nina pressed Neka in her arms, but both knew the danger that lay in wait for them.

Then suddenly, they were startled by the sound of twigs. Nina looked in the nearby bush, but could see no one. For the past few days, she felt that someone had been following her. Nina could not put anything past Ada and the chief. His aides were everywhere. He may have ordered some of them to follow her to make sure that Neka would not be smuggled out of town.

Chapter 9

The sunset had faded over the hills, and the moon was not yet up. Two solitary stars shone like warning lights in the deep blue sky. The wind blew against the trees, and sounds of wild animals could be heard all around, as if complaining of the approaching nightfall. Nina waited until darkness fell fully over the hills. Staying in the shadows, she took the pathway through the forest to the small harbor, shielding her face with a silk scarf which she wore like a hood. In the distance she could see a fading lantern at the fish market as closing time neared. Guided by the distant light from the fish market on the east bank, she approached the harbor on silent feet. She watched as the last passenger was ferried across the lake. Only a tall woman remained.

"Could you take me across?" Nina asked. She turned her face slightly to avoid recognition, while offering the woman two naira, the usual cost for a ride across the lake.

"Sure," the woman answered, without looking at Nina. She steadied the large boat, and looked on as Nina pulled her dress up to her ankles in the shallow water and climbed into the boat. The woman began to row the boat across the lake, which was relatively calm. A slight shift in the direction of the wind, and Nina caught a whiff of the woman's perfume. She found it odd. It was the scent that hung in the air during burials, which as a child she had feared. Suddenly there was a loud splash in the water, and the boat began swaying violently. The woman had tossed her paddles overboard. A horrible suspicion sprang to Nina's mind.

The blood surged in her head. She looked around, she was yards from shore, and she couldn't swim! The woman turned, grabbed Nina by the throat, and with a sudden push nearly had her in the lake. The boat rocked violently, but Nina held on, and a desperate struggle began. With almost superhuman strength, the woman hurled Nina overboard, but Nina clung to the woman and managed to take her as well into the water. Now they both clung to the side of the boat. Nina saw through the light that reflected from the fish market that her antagonist was none other than Ada! Her new fears gave her an added surge of adrenalin. She struck Ada a vicious blow with her elbow, and Ada released her grip on the boat. Nina then, somehow, lifted herself into the boat. Sensing that Ada was tiring, she knelt forward, seized Ada by the hair and the throat, and submerged her in the water. Ada thrashed the water violently, but Nina did not release her grip until the lake grew quiet.

Nina collapsed, exhausted. Thoughts flowed through her mind. Although she was sure that the chief had sent spies after her, she couldn't understand how they could have informed Ada that she would be at the lake at that particular time. Unless...

The nurses--one of them could be a spy for the chief. After all, they were natives. It was only natural that they should take orders from him.

The full moon was now rising. The boat had drifted to the shore. Nina looked around and found a set of oars. In the distance, she could hear the voices of men at the fish market as she rowed the boat toward a deserted part of the market. Her arms ached and she struggled desperately to keep the boat on course. Within minutes, she reached the market. As she climbed ashore, the voices of men came to her from a hovel. It was the only bar open. On one side of the hut, the last merchants were walking to their boats to make the trip across. Nina remained in the shadows. Within minutes she saw Uloma creep closer, carrying a bag in one hand and her baby in the other arm. Nina watched as Uloma set her bag down gently in her little boat, and then climbed in with her baby. A bright light shone onto the lake through the small window of the hut, when someone, hearing the splash from Uloma's paddle, lifted the curtain. Nina heard the man say something, and leave the hut. Moments later, he appeared. He looked carefully around, then hurriedly boarded a boat and paddled quickly after Uloma.

Nina's heart beat in her throat. She knew if something went wrong, no one would be around to rescue her. Nevertheless, after the man disappeared from view, she rushed to her boat and trailed after him, keeping sight of the slight wake from his boat. All but exhausted, Nina reached the deserted bank of the lake, climbed out of the boat, and made her way up the hill onto the rocky outcrop where she had sat a week before. She hurriedly unzipped her waterproof waistbag and brought out the tiny night camera Dr. Lloyd had left with her. Energized by the adrenalin that flowed through her, she crept down the steep, then through the ravine. She dropped down onto the nearby grass above the cliff. By raising her head she had a view of the man as he approached Uloma, laughing stridently.

"Come on, you mad girl, you know you like it." A slap tore across Uloma's face. Startled by the blow, her baby began to cry. Nina closed her eyes. She felt impelled to intervene, but she knew she had to stay out of it if she were to expose the man and his actions. No one would believe her without concrete evidence.

"Why are you doing this to me?" Uloma cried.

"You know no one wants you," the man said. "You should feel lucky to have me." Then he ripped the wrapper from around her waist. Instinctively, Uloma laid her baby down in the grass for safety. As she rose, Nina saw the man lift her off her feet and carry her through the narrow pathway into the ravine. With trembling hands, Nina pressed the shutter, catching the scene on film. Uloma kicked and pounded on the man's chest, but the man's grip was vicelike. Lowering her head, she sank her teeth into the man's arm. The man let out a loud scream. Nina's hand again pressed the shutter on the camera. The moon was almost as clear as day.

"You damned mad girl!" he screamed as he released Uloma, then he began cursing at the pain. "You damned bitch. You bit me."

Uloma made a mad dash for her baby, but with one drunken leap, the man caught her and again wrestled her to the ground. He pinned her down, and landed another vicious blow on her face. Nina managed several more camera shots, but wished the horrible ordeal were over. For several moments the forest grew quiet. Only the roaring waters from the waterfall could be heard far off.

"Please, don't hit me anymore." Uloma was subdued by the violence and the noise of her baby crying.

"Then you must do as I say," the man ordered. He continued to rape her, and Uloma's moans synchronized with her baby's. The time that it took the man to finish seemed like an eternity. Nina picked up a large stone from the ravine and threw it next to the man. Startled, he released Uloma and fled down the narrow path clutching his clothes. Nina waited until the man disappeared into the valley, then rose from the grass and walked several yards to where Uloma's baby lay crying. She took the baby in her arms, and went to Uloma, who lay dazed from the attack.

"I'm so sorry I couldn't stop him," Nina said contritely, helping Uloma to her feet. "He would have attacked me too, if I had intervened, and I wouldn't have been able to do what I did do." She handed Uloma what remained of her wrapper, and helped her to cover her waist. "But I have the evidence to have this man punished. You no longer will suffer in his hands."

"No one can stop him," Uloma said, in a child's hopeless voice.

"I promise, I will," Nina insisted. Then she heard a splash on the lake, and turning her head she saw what looked like a figure running towards her. She handed Uloma her baby. "Here, take your bag and go at once," Nina whispered. Turning again to look at the figure, something flashed across her face. The impact sent fire through her body. The forest seemed to reel around her, and she fought to keep on her feet. Seeing an object coming at her, she held up her hand, but too late. The impact drove her backward, and she tripped over a large stone. She looked up to see Ada standing over her.

"You're as good as dead, you harlot," Ada roared. Her hand rose and fell evenly as she struck Nina in the face with some object. Nina's face was contorted with the pain, but she saw that Ada's finger was reaching behind her neck, the fingernail looking like an eagle's claw. Nina kicked Ada solidly in the groin. Ada fell backward violently. Rising quickly to her feet, Nina sprinted down the path towards the road. She knew she couldn't fight Ada. One scratch from her poison dart, and it would be the end. She felt her waistbag, her camera was still in place. She was sure Ada had not witnessed the man rape Uloma, but she couldn't understand how the woman had escaped drowning--how she seemed to be everywhere.

When Nina finally reached the hospital, the candle was still flickering in its wooden platter in the hallway. Despite her orders, her aide slept like a log. Nina didn't disturb the nurse, but poured cold water in a small basin, and hands trembling, began to wash her face. The scratches on her face stung. She looked at herself in the mirror. There was a swelling where Ada had hit her, and her shirt was torn in several places. She applied first aid to her wounds, then sat in a chair and began taking off her shoes.

After a spell, her thoughts turned to the future. She knew that the next day she would have to surrender Neka to the chief, and she did not know what would become of her. She looked through the glass louver and saw a dull light burning from a lantern in Neka's room. Neither Neka nor the nuns would ever know how close to death she came that evening at the lake. Ada would have drowned her, and no one would have known what had happened. Now, the only thing left was to uncover Uloma's rapist and save Neka from death.

Chapter 10

Nina tossed and turned, trying fruitlessly to catch a few hours of sleep. She had to be ready if she were to defend Neka adequately. She stared at the underside of the corrugated tin roof, her mind flooded with thoughts of Ada and the man who had raped Uloma. A mosquito flew across the room. She rose and spotted the insect as it perched on a crossbeam. With one slap, the mosquito fell to the floor. It whined and circled the floor in an attempt to take flight. Nina quickly stepped on it, and blood squirted out. She couldn't stand seeing a mosquito before she fell asleep, knowing that once she closed her eyes she would be bitten,followed by two weeks of malaria, a terrible illness. Ironically, even though the victim couldn't keep warm the body temperature reached 104 degrees. Accompanying this were the uncontrollable cold chills, dry mouth, nausea, vomiting, and jaundice--and even death. Moments later, Nina fell asleep, but she dreamed the same thoughts that had kept her awake.

"Open the door!" a man's voice yelled. Nina drifted between consciousness and deep sleep. The pounding on her door blended with her dreams until a hand shook her. Startled, she drew up the covers sharply.

"There are men at the door, doctor," the nurse said. Nina looked at the clock on the wooden stand. It was two o'clock in the morning. Just then, Sister Brooke and Sister Kristin walked into her room.

"Here, I need you to go to the film lab at Owerri first thing this morning." Nina thought quickly, and handed the films to Sister Brooke. She knew, however, that it took at least three days to have the special film developed. It would not be enough time to make the pictures available.

"Have them print several copies of the negatives. I don't have much time to explain." Sister Brooke disappeared into her bedroom with the negatives, but reappeared moments later at the shouts of a man.

"Open the door, I said!" Nina's heart pounded against her ribs. She saw the fear on the nuns' faces. The men began to ram the door and it started to crash.

"What is it that you want!" Nina yelled as the door opened. Mazi Igwe was standing in front of her. His face was painted with traditional white chalk. He had tied a fresh palm leaf around his head, which contributed to the warrior look. Behind Mazi Igwe was his ten-man entourage. They had colored their faces in the same fashion. It presaged the slaying of a villain or the burial of a suicide.

"Where is she?" Mazi Igwe asked.

"They aren't supposed to hold the trial until noon," Nina said. "You've already tricked me. Neka can't get a fair trial right now! How could the trial take place while the town is asleep? You're not being fair. You just want her dead."

"This is the way it has always been done," Mazi Igwe responded. "It has been passed down by our great-grandfathers. Now, hand the thief over or we will seize her by force."

"You don't have to come looking for me." The voice sounded behind Mazi Igwe. Nina saw Neka emerge from the shadows behind the crowd. Immediately, she was surrounded by Mazi Igwe's men. "I'm an innocent woman," Neka continued. "I'm not afraid to go before the chief. God has my end in view. He sees everything--things beyond our thoughts and imagination. You took my children from me, now you want my life. You must answer to the Great Ruler of all things." Neka looked at Nina, and smiled pensively. "I know how you feel, Princess, but this is a journey I'll have to make by myself. This might be the time God grants me to reunite with my children."

"Nonsense," Nina said. "I can't let you appear before the chief alone. I'm coming with you."

Neka paused. She met Nina's gaze. "The last thing I want you to witness is my death, Princess. You have nothing to proffer in my defense. And even if you do, they won't believe you. No, you must remain behind and continue to fight for your cause. Our children need you. In spite of it all, I have led a good life. God has made me happy."

"Don't speak in that manner, Mama," Nina said. "When have I known you to give up hope?" Nina's eyes were filled with tears, her lips fluttering uncontrollably.

"You have nothing to fear," Sister Brooke interjected. "God is on your side."

*   *   *

Neka was led through the unpaved road toward the market square. Nina heard the tom-tom sound of the village drum. She looked at her watch, it was three o'clock in the morning. This time, the town didn't appear. Nina knew the coded sounds of the drum. Women, children, and untitled elders weren't summoned by this call, only a few titled elders and the young men honored for their heroism and valor. Though a few children slept through the sound, Nina remembered that when she was a little girl she would often be filled with dread when she heard the beat of the drums. She remembered how a threat seemed to hang in the air like thick smoke, as if someone might smash through the door and take her mother and father away. It was a fear she carried throughout adolescence.

The moon was perched high over the western hilltops. Several stars blinked far away in space. Not a single cloud marked the sky. A mild wind in the cool of the night blew, showering them with silver dew and creating a false sense of ease. An eerie silence hung in the air, except for the muffled footsteps of the men on the sandy road. Nina could see the chief's compound on the top of a small hill. It appeared different in the moonlight. It looked like a large anthill surrounded by smaller trees, or large mushrooms over a recently manicured field.

Nina looked at Neka. Neka's pace suddenly slowed, and she began talking furiously with herself in a dramatic monologue, a sign of her returning illness. One of the men prodded Neka with a wooden club, pushing her forward.

"Hurry up," Mazi Igwe said. "We don't have much time. The elders can't be kept waiting."

Nina ran forward. "Enough of this! You assaulted her at the market, and got away with it. This time, you won't."

"The woman is a thief and as such deserves no dignified treatment." Just then, voices were heard over the walls of the chief's compound. Nina, too, feared the events that were about to take place, afraid that this could be the last day she would see Neka alive.

*   *   *

The chief was seated in the semicircle of the titled elders. Like Mazi Igwe, their faces were colored in traditional white chalk, their necks in red clay. As Nina and Neka walked in, all eyes were on them, some pretending to be congenial, some grim. She knew this was truly a day of reckoning. She never thought the elders could put such fear in her. The silence in the courtyard was so total that they could hear each other breathe. She and Neka stopped in front of the chief, went down on their knees, and touched the ground with their foreheads, a ritual greeting that Nina resented. But she felt if she went along with the tradition, she might possibly soften the chief's and the elders' hearts and spare Neka's life.

"Lead her to the pedestal," the chief said. Mazi Igwe took Neka by the arm and led her to a wooden platform just below the chief's chair. Chief Eze gave Nina a piercing look, she felt only distrust for him.

"It's unfortunate that our meeting today may not end well for you and your friend," the chief said. "I realize how you and Neka must feel, knowing that you have been ordered to face the elders, but I assure you that this trial will be fair and just."

Nina swallowed hard and cleared her throat. She knew there was no truth in Chief Eze's words. Neka's position was precarious at best, but she determined that, somehow, she would turn the event in Neka's favor.

"We are only following the laws set forth by our great-grandfathers," Chief Eze continued. "The punishment for stealing is death. If Neka pleads not guilty and is found guilty, she will die, and her body will be given to the oracle of the hills. If she confesses to her crime, her life will be spared, but she will be banished as an Osu--an outcast of the town. For all of her life she will be forbidden to interact with any one of us. If she had children, her children and their future children would not be allowed to marry our citizens, but have to marry an Osu. But it will be up to the elders to decide her guilt. If she is found innocent, our town will celebrate. Now, could you tell us what happened, Neka?"

Nina pondered over what the chief had just said. She could ask Neka to confess and save her life. Yes, she would be an outcast, but she had no children to suffer with her. But Nina mistrusted the elders. She wasn't sure what punishment they would in fact recommend. And she knew she would never forgive herself if she were to convince Neka to confess to a crime she hadn't committed, only to be punished anyway. Another thought came to Nina.

"Pardon me, Chief Eze," Nina interjected. "Isn't Neka allowed to confront her accuser? All this time she has been treated as a thief, not a single soul has stood as her accuser."

"We are aware of this, but a thief might want to confess before we ask her accuser to come forward." Just then, the double gates of the chief's compound sprang open. In

132

walked Ada with a younger woman. The elders stared at Ada, their eyes like a circle of pointed arrows. Nina rose to her feet. She felt sick. She knew immediately that Neka was slated to be framed. The silence was finally broken by Ada's voice.

"Here is her accuser," Ada said, pointing to the young woman, and stood planted in front of the chief. She was the only woman who never greeted the chief in the traditional manner. But Neka's accuser went on her knees before the chief, and touched the ground with her forehead.

"Now that we have Neka's accuser, we must proceed quickly," Chief Eze said. He looked at the woman. "Now, young lady, would you tell us what happened?"

Nina, studying the woman, could sense her inner conflict. The woman really didn't want to be there; her eyes darted back and forth from Ada to the chief. "Master, I was selling children's clothing at the market when that woman standing over there came from behind me and grabbed a handful of cloth. Someone saw her and summoned help. They retrieved the pieces of cloth from her and gave them back to me." The woman stared at Ada, as if to determine whether she had done a good job.

Nina was shaken.

> *Could it be true that Neka really stole from the market? I remember seeing several baby garments on her children's graves. Could it be that her illness led her to steal for her children?*

"Who was that person who summoned help?" Mazi Igwe asked. "Is he or she amongst us?"

133

"I...I don't know his name. He got mixed up with the crowd."

"It doesn't matter who saw her steal," Ada said. "The woman is a thief, and she should die like one."

Chief Eze coughed, as if to clear his throat of a sudden tightness. "Now, Neka, what do you have to say to your accuser?"

Neka stood woodenly on the platform and didn't utter a word. She stared off into the distance as if to absent herself from the events around her.

"Listen, please, Neka is a periodic mad woman," Nina said. "We can't ignore the fact and convict her of a crime she doesn't even know happened. I can prove to you not only that she didn't steal from the market, but that she is being framed by the woman before you. Just hours ago she tried to drown me in the lake."

"I won't tolerate such rubbish," Chief Eze said, and stood up angrily, his hand waving in Nina's face. Nina was somewhat taken aback, but not totally intimidated. "You won't stop at anything, will you?" he continued. "Just a few months ago you accused Ada of poisoning you. This is a trial of a woman who stole from the market. She must answer for herself or I will have no option but to deliver her to the oracle of the hills. Now, if you will allow this proceeding to continue."

"But if an innocent woman is killed, and delivered to the oracle, her spirit will forever haunt our town," Nina said pensively.

"That is a chance we will all have to take. Ada's reputation is unassailable." Chief Eze waved his hand around to urge

134

the elders to continue.

Nina spotted something dishonest in Chief Eze's body language and facial expressions. Something was wrong.

"Wait," Ada said. "I have a proposition to make. We are willing to forgive Neka's crime if you, Nina, agree to refrain from teaching the abolition of female circumcision."

Nina looked at the chief; there was a smirk on his face. Only Mazi Igwe seemed baffled at Ada's suggestion. Nina felt sick to her stomach. She couldn't believe that the hostilities against her and her reforms had reached such fever pitch. Obviously these people would stop at nothing.

"I have a counter-proposition," Nina said. She looked at her watch; it was now after four in the morning. Sister Brooke and Sister Kristin must have left for Owerri to develop the negatives, but she needed a few more days to have the films printed. "Listen, it's not Neka that you want. You want me. You are simply trying to get at me through her. If you agree to render the same punishment you threaten Neka with to the man who got Uloma, the mad girl, pregnant, not only will I stop my teachings, I will leave this town forever."

"And how are you going to find this man?" the chief asked, taking a quick look and smiling at Ada.

"I promise that I will deliver this man to you in three days, with proof, but you must assure me of one thing."

The chief eyed Nina suspiciously. "And what is that?"

"This man must be tried in front of the whole town."

"And if you are wrong, both you and Neka will face the same fate as you wish for this man?" Ada added with an unamused smile.

Nina paused for a moment, and looked at Neka. Neka still gazed in the distance. Nina felt uncertain. She didn't want to be responsible for Neka's death. But she knew what Neka's answer would have been, giving her hatred of Ada. She shut her eyes for a moment, then blurted out, "Yes. But only on one condition. If I'm right, you will face the same fate as Neka and I for sacrificing her twins to the gods of the forest. Do you agree?"

Ada's gaze met the chief's. Chief Eze nodded.

"I agree," Ada said.

"You do realize the punishment for both of you will be death?" Chief Eze said, glowing with satisfaction at how Nina had been cornered. "The trial will be held at the shrine of the oracle. No convicted person has ever made it out of the gorge."

Nina thought grimly of the stories she had heard of the gorge as a child:

> *Those convicted of crimes are blindfolded,*
> *and are made to walk along a narrow rocky*
> *ledge until they miss their footing, and drop*
> *two hundred feet into the roaring torrent of*
> *the gorge.*

"I do realize this, chief," Nina said. "But I pity you both. My laugh will come last."

The chief looked at Mazi Igwe. "I need you to summon the whole town in three days at the first light of dawn. We will all meet at the foothills of Umueze."

"One more thing," Nina said. "You must allow me to visit the gorge. This will enable me to make peace with the oracle of the hills."

"You may do as you wish, because you are going to need it," Ada interjected. "And watch your step. It's a bad omen to fall into the gorge before the trail."

"I pity you," Nina said. "This time none of your cronies will come to your aid. The whole town will know you for what you are--a thief, and a murderer of children."

The chief laughed sardonically, as if enjoying Nina and Ada's verbal fencing. "Now that you both have shown that you're ready to put your lives on the line to satisfy your honor, why not end this affair amicably?"

"I'm willing," Nina said. But Ada seemed sure of herself. Her face shone with satisfaction at the possibility to deliver Nina and Neka to the oracle of the hills. She said nothing. Nina began leading Neka towards the double gates of the compound.

"Wait," Ada said. Nina turned, and looked on as Ada and the chief whispered together for a long moment. Then Ada turned and continued, "My conditions are these: You make an immediate public withdrawal of your slander and your teachings, and apologize to me personally, and we will let you and Neka get on with your lives."

"I can't believe such impudence! Let me assure you that you have more to worry about than I."

"Then, you will die," Ada said.

Nina shrugged her shoulders. "My laugh will come last."

*   *   *

Nina walked away from Chief Eze's compound, aware

of the uncertainty she had planted in their minds. She left Neka at the hospital, hoping that the medicine she had given her would keep her illness in abeyance before the trial. After a mile walk through the forest, she reached the foothill of Umueze. She could hear the warning calls of animals all around her. She made her way through a narrow path uphill, and a short distance later arrived at a rocky clearing. The forest licked her body, dampening her with the cool mist that had fallen on the leaves the night before. On her right was a sheer cliff, a tottering natural stairway of broken rocks. Clinging to the bushes, she scrambled up the slope, her heart beating against her chest. She crossed over a narrow shelf, and moments later she was standing on a ledge covered with white sand. She had reached the sheer cliff of the gorge.

She went to the edge and looked down. Her head reeled. The drop into the gorge was filled with jagged, moss-covered rocks, which had aged with time and storms. It was clear why no one had survived a fall into the gorge. But she wanted to visit this place which had claimed dozens of lives. If she and Neka were forced to fall into the gorge, she would at least have assured herself there were no means of escape. She wasn't worried for herself. But she wanted, if possible to find an escape route for Neka.

As she turned to leave, she held onto a tree branch to lift herself onto a ledge. She lost her footing, and a rush of rocks went hurtling down the slope and the branch snapped. She slid down the slope but managed to stop her fall by grabbing a rocky ledge.

She hung with her back to the precipice. If she lost her

grip, she would slide down the gorge and into the roaring torrent below. Gently, she lifted one foot onto the ledge. Her face was beaded with sweat, and she was tired from lack of sleep. But with one more huge effort, she lifted the rest of her body. Reaching a flat rocky clearing, she dropped in exhaustion.

No one, she was sure, would come to save her and Neka if things went badly for them. She had committed her life to stopping female circumcision and the injustice dealt the underprivileged in her town, and because of it she feared that she might lose one of the most important friends in her life.

Suddenly she felt strange. The warning calls of animals had ceased, replaced by the tom-tom of the town's drum, as if beckoning the town and calling her name. She shook her head to clear it of confusion. Her mind was playing tricks on her. Imagining the danger she faced was slowly robbing her of her senses. She wasn't sure whether she and Neka would survive the next few days.

Chapter 11

When Nina reached the hospital from the forest, Sister Brooke and Sister Kristin were waiting for her in the small veranda facing the garden. They rose from their *agada* chairs as Nina approached. This had been Nina's third visit to the gorge of the oracle in the last three days. It was strange, but she found the gorge and the surrounding forest fascinating and full of mystery.

"These are horrible pictures, Nina," Sister Brooke said, pointing to the photos she had had developed, shaking her head in disbelief. "What animal is this man? Poor Uloma, I can't believe that a normal human being could do this to a mad woman." She handed the envelope containing the pictures to Nina.

"I'm sorry that I had to ask you to have these films developed, but this is my only chance of exposing the man and his iniquities. With these pictures in hand, I can show the good I'm trying to achieve, whereas if I'm shunned by the town, nothing can be done." She took the pictures out of the envelope and looked at them. Although a little dark, they revealed the identity of the man, and his actions. She felt a glimmer of triumph, followed quickly by a feeling of sadness. If the town believed her, she and Neka would live, but if they rejected her, she would not only die, but so would Neka, which was her greatest fear.

She looked through the window onto the dusty road, and heard the tom-tom call of the drum. A throng of people--men, women, and children--were walking towards the chief's compound. In just a few minutes, the trial would begin at the shrine of the oracle, and her fate would be decided by those who hated her. Her face was beaded with sweat from nervousness, she felt nauseous, and her stomach churned. But if the town came to understand her motives, she would be honored, and her cause would conquer ignorance and superstition.

She looked at her friends. "I know what you're thinking. But I believe I will have to make this journey on my own. These people will stop at nothing. If you try to support me, your very lives might be in danger. In fact, your mere presence might make matters worse, feeling as they do about foreigners interfering in their affairs. Moreover, if things go badly for me, the children will need you more than ever here at the hospital."

Nina's eyes filled with tears as she spoke. She hugged the nuns in turn. Nina felt awkward when she saw Sister Brooke begin to recite the Rosary. But the sight made her realize that she might never see Sister Brooke and Sister Kristin again. She took in a deep breath and closed her eyes for a long moment. Her thoughts were on the roaring current rushing through the gorge, and the clap of the waterfall as the waters slammed against the jagged rocks. The words of her mother echoed in her mind, as if she were hearing them for the first time:

The villain is blindfolded and is led over a —

footing, and plummets two hundred feet into the
gorge. His body is mauled by the jagged rocks as
he falls into the torrents. In most cases, the body
is not found for days because it wedges against
the rocks, and when finally found, it floats onto
the lake, bloated from decay.

Nina and Neka walked through a path in the forest, avoiding the regular lime walk. Although the sun was out, mist continued to collect on leaves and trees, most of it blown by the wind from the torrents. They walked silently through the fringe of the lake; each knew what the other was thinking, but neither spoke. The tall iroko at the base of the shrine of the oracle grew larger as they approached and the forest animals became quiet, as if subdued by the noise from the crowd. The animals even seemed to know. After all, they had witnessed such proceedings from time immemorial.

All eyes fell on Nina and Neka as they approached. The noisy crowd stilled. The bushes around the shrine were almost hidden by all the town's people. In the clearing, some sat on long benches, some on wooden *agada* chairs which they had brought with them, while others perched on smaller trees around the shrine for a better view. They fidgeted, pointed at Nina and Neka, and spoke softly among themselves.

The elders, their eyelids still marked in the traditional white chalk, their necks in red clay, sat in a semicircle in front of the chief at their center, while Ada and Neka's accuser stood on a small pedestal next to the shrine. Nina led Neka to a smaller pedestal in the middle of the shrine. The scent of an old sacrifice spewed from the shrine, filling the air with a scent, like a camel's breath. Foul taste filled her mouth, followed by a rush of saliva. Turning away, she tried to spit it out.

The chief walked to the center of the crowd and pierced the people with his hawk-like eyes. It was the malicious look that always made Nina mistrust him. She clutched the envelope that contained the pictures of the rapist in her hand.

"People of Eze, I have gathered you here for another hearing. The last time this type of trial was held, I thought I would never see another one in my lifetime. It was when Egonna killed Ezeigbo. The trial lasted for one week, but I assure you that this one will not. Within the next few hours, the villains will be exposed, and you can return to your homes, your farms, or the market. Of course, those of you who wish to witness the convicted women turned over to the oracle of the hills may do so. Now, I would like to ask Mazi Igwe to pass around the kola nut."

Chief Eze sat down and waited for the ritual passing of the kola nut. First, Mazi Igwe reverently offered the kola nut to the chief in a small tray. Chief Eze didn't take it, but placed his hand over the tray and recited the usual prayer. "He who brings kola nut, brings life. May we be guided by the spirits of our great-grandfathers always to make the right judgments. May their spirits guard us against disease and the evil spirits that may afflict our town." Everyone chimed in with an "Amen."

Nina and Neka were the only ones who refused the kola nut. Nina looked at Neka, whose color had returned to her face and who seemed to be more coherent than before.

Evidently the medicine Nina had given her had taken effect. Neka was more aware of her surroundings and recognized almost everyone. The crowd suddenly hushed as Chief Eze again stood up from his chair.

"My people, we must proceed quickly," Chief Eze said, and stood in front of the elders. "Let me begin by saying that, although this is not the first time we have gone through such a difficult proceeding, many of us will be saddened by the events that will take place today. The last thing any of us would like is to lose one of our brothers or sisters. But we must be courageous in dealing with the crimes of robbery. Our very livelihoods are threatened by them. Should we not check the actions of thieves, our weakness would encourage others to do likewise, which would bring anarchy to our town. Therefore, their actions must not go unpunished. We must deal with them mercilessly. Anyone who comes to their aid in obstructing justice must be dealt the same fate.

"Now, let us begin this difficult trial. I would like to call Mazi Igwe to be our moderator. This is a position he has previously filled fairly, for he is a man of justice."

"Thank you, Chief Eze," Mazi Igwe said. He turned to the elders. "Thank you too for granting me the privilege of standing before you." He looked at the crowd, then at Nina and Neka. "And, thank you all for dropping everything you had to do this morning to answer the chief. As I look around, I don't think there is any man, woman or child missing from our town. You have responded just as you've always done. Our town is a great town.

"Now that we begin this difficult journey, we must all realize that our decisions are permanent. The accused will

145

have the right to confront his or her accuser and to call witnesses or have someone speak in his or her defense. Those of you who have been called as witnesses must be truthful. Remember, the punishment for bearing false witness is death. Also remember that our honor is at stake. Our trial will be in two parts. First, we have Neka's trial. Secondly, we have to determine whether Nina can identify the man who got Uloma, the mad girl, pregnant."

The crowd roared and broke into talk.

"Quiet! Please," Mazi Igwe yelled. Gradually the noise subsided except for the occasional coughs. "If Nina accuses the wrong man of this crime, her penalty will be death. But if Nina is right, Ada, who challenged Nina to produce this man, will be given to the oracle of the hills for offering Neka's twins to the gods of the forest. This was agreed between the two of them and witnessed by the chief and the elders. People of Eze, we have never had a trial of this nature, one where two women have challenged each other with their lives.

"This trial can be halted if both women agree to withdraw their challenges and leave us with Neka's trial," Mazi Igwe continued.

"Now, Nina, will you agree to withdraw your challenge?"

Nina looked at Ada and the chief. Chief Eze winked at Ada, thinking Nina would be backing out. But, surprisingly, Ada was pale and uncertain. She looked at Nina directly for the first time since their arrival. Nina sensed Ada was troubled, but she knew pride would keep her from saving her own life.

"I'm willing," Nina said, trying to win sympathy from

the crowd.

"Ada, what do you say?" Mazi Igwe asked.

"How dare you suggest that I withdraw my challenge to a villain," Ada said. "This woman is a harlot and has taught our children her evil ways. We might as well forgive Neka for her crime, but then it would be a great injustice to those convicted, and to those who died in the past for committing this crime. What type of people are we, if we can't even uphold our own laws?"

Nina shook her head; Ada had obviously banished her doubts.

"Then we must continue this trial without any more ado," Mazi Igwe said and turned to the woman next to Ada. "Now, Ekema, will you tell us what happened at the market?" For the first time, Mazi Igwe called Neka's accuser by name. The mention of it sparked Nina's memory. She wasn't that much older than Nina. Ekema and she had played as children at the runoff of the waterfall two miles from the lake. Moreover, Ekema's mother had been a lifelong friend of Neka's before her death.

Ekema's gaze met Nina's as she walked to the front of the elders and the chief. Nina sensed Ekema's turmoil. She didn't want to be there. Ekema went on her knees and touched her forehead to the ground in the ritual reverence. Then she walked back to the pedestal and began: "I was selling children's clothing at the market when Neka came from behind me and grabbed a handful of items. Someone saw her and summoned help. Several people came to my aid and were able to subdue her and retrieve the stolen items. This is all I know."

147

Nina looked at Neka. She was listening to Ekema's words and shaking her head in bewilderment. Nina gave Neka a reassuring pat, waiting for Mazi Igwe to call her. The crowd was silent. The sun had appeared over the horizon, and a gentle wind blew from the valley, rustling the bushes around the shrine and sending a soft scent through the air.

"Now, Neka, are you aware of any reason why Ekema would make a false accusation against you?" Mazi Igwe asked, looking hard at Neka. "You may also give us your own account of the event at the market."

"I will take up Neka's defense," Nina said.

"No!" Ada yelled. "That's against the rules." She looked at the chief inquiringly. Chief Eze for a moment looked baffled but then said, "She must conduct her own defense."

"But it has been customary for a close friend to come to the defense of the accused," Nina objected, looking at Mazi Igwe.

"Not in this case," Ada shouted.

"Both of you, be quiet!" Mazi Igwe yelled angrily. "You are also on trial, Ada. You gave up your right to dictate what happens in this forum when you became a defendant." He looked at the chief. "The right to chair trials has been passed to my family by our great-grandfathers. We have always been a family that adheres to justice. No one can change the rules. Nina may speak."

"Well then, young lady, you may continue," Mazi Igwe said, looking at Nina.

Nina went to stand in front of the elders. She saw Ada look at the chief, thwarted by Mazi Igwe. The chief shrugged and gave a forced smile. Ada walked to the chief in confusion and they whispered for a long moment, as if Ada was seeking reassurance from the chief. Then they parted.

"My fellow people of Eze, the accusation which Ekema has made is simply not so," Nina said. "If any of you believes Neka is a thief, please speak up. She has nothing left in this world but her dignity of being human. And even this has been challenged since the onset of her illness.

"As a young woman, she was obedient to her parents and did all that was required of a young woman in our community. She was sent into servitude at the tender age of ten in order to repay her father's debt. Like many of our women, she was subjected to years of rape by her master's son. Eventually, he got her pregnant at the age of fifteen. Out of respect for her father, she married a man whom she did not love, but whom she grew to love from necessity. She has always been a hard-working woman, no one can say otherwise.

"Then as a young woman, God blessed her with twins on three occasions, but Ada took them and gave them to the gods of the forest. Time cannot heal this wound in her heart. As I look through the crowd, I see other women who have also lost their children."

Tears ran down Neka's cheeks as she listened to Nina speak. Many of the women in the crowd had tears in their eyes as well.

"Ekema comes from an honorable family," Nina continued. "Neka has always treated her like a daughter. Ekema's mother also had twins, and her babies too were given to the gods of the forest by the woman who stands

149

beside her. Ekema is alive today because she was born a single child. If she had been born a twin, she would have died at the hands of that woman."

Nina, staring at Ekema, could sense her agitation. "Ekema, your mother and father, like many parents in our town, died of grief because Ada delivered your brothers and sisters to the gods of the forest. I used to see you sitting under the iroko tree as a child, alone and lonely. The other children wouldn't play with you because they thought you were different. But I played with you. There was nothing wrong with you. In another coincidence, like Neka, your mother, before her death, was stricken with grief, mentally tormented by the woman who pretends to be your friend. Your mother and father are uneasy in their graves, seeing what you are about to do to an innocent woman. I challenge you to stand in front of our people, look at Neka, and call her a thief. Please tell the truth and admit that Neka is an honorable woman."

Nina looked at the crowd. Some stood on their feet to get a better view, while the shorter ones jostled to get to the front. Nina stared at Ekema with some sympathy. Ekema was clearly burdened by her conscience. Her eyes darted from the chief to Ada for support, but they seemed unable to give any. For a moment, Nina thought Ada would actually apologize to the crowd. Her face showed a mixture of expressions. Nina had put her in a dangerous position. No one had ever dared challenge Ada in any way, but now Ada had to convince the crowd that Nina's words were false-- and she couldn't do it.

"Ekema!" Nina yelled. "For the sake of justice, I would

like you to look at the crowd and tell them straight out that Neka is a thief!"

Tears poured down Ekema's face. She was petrified with fear. The chief stood up angrily. "You cannot intimidate this young woman and force her to retract her accusation. She saw Neka steal from the market, and that's all there is to it."

"With all due respect, Chief Eze, I'm in charge of this trial," Mazi Igwe said. "I decide when a witness is threatened. And I declare that no one is above justice. If I wrongfully flogged these two women in the market because I believed one of them was a thief, and the other came to her aid, then I was wrong. There is no other way to redress my actions than to give them a fair trial. My position as a moderator is backed by the crowd in front of you, not by you or Ada. I owe it to them to ensure that justice is done. In the final analysis, they will be the judges. They will decide who lives, and who dies."

Nina could not believe her ears. It was as if she was dreaming. Ekema stood in front of the elders and looked at Neka. Then Ekema's head dropped. Nina sensed Neka wanted to open her arms to Ekema and reassure her that everything would be all right. Suddenly, Ekema turned to the crowd with fear-filled eyes.

"I hope you will find it in your hearts to forgive me," she said. Her lips trembled, her voice was contrite. "Neka is not a thief--far from it. She has been like a mother to me. She is a very kind woman. I have ignored my conscience, and strained all decency by calling her a thief. It was a terrible mistake to side with those who wanted her and Nina dead, and I hope that you will find it in your hearts to forgive me."

Nina watched as the women in the crowd wiped the tears from their faces with their wrappers, while the men stared with compassion.

"But why did you do it?" Mazi Igwe asked, looking at Ekema.

"Because Ada made me."

Mazi Igwe looked at the elders, then at the crowd. "Which one of you believes Neka is guilty?" No one spoke. The silence hung thick in the air.

Ada's eyes darted from the crowd to the chief. Her lips were dry and trembling. It was as if her world had blown apart in front of her. Ada walked over to the chief, they began talking furiously. Then the chief threw up his hands, and said quite loudly, "You are a fool. You wanted her dead. Now you're the one who will die if you don't listen to me."

Nina didn't think the crowd heard the chief's words. For a moment she thought once again that Ada would apologize to the crowd, but then realized that Ada was counting on Chief Eze to intervene on her behalf.

Nina turned to Ekema. "Thank you, Ekema, for your courageous admission," Nina said, and watched as Ekema joined the crowd. Several woman hugged Ekema. Ada stood alone on the pedestal, her eyes darting like a leopard in distress.

Mazi Igwe looked at the elders who seemed confused. The shock on their faces was evident. "I must remind you that the punishment for bearing false witness is death," Mazi Igwe said, looking at Ada. "In this case, the young woman Ekema was driven to do so. Therefore, we must find the pity in our hearts to forgive her. But the one who is responsible for inciting her must not go unpunished."

Nina looked at Ada, whose face was pale and sullen. "I'll give you one more chance to confess your sins to the crowd," Nina said. "If you do not, you will be given to the oracle of the hills, but if you confess, the crowd will show mercy."

"Let me remind you that we didn't come here to hear confessions," Mazi Igwe said, looking at Nina. "You were challenged to expose the man who impregnated Uloma, the mad girl. Should you fail to do so, you also will be given to the oracle of the hills."

A noise from the back drew the attention of the crowd. They turned and saw Uloma, carrying her baby and walking to the front of the shrine. She walked directly to Nina, and the baby reached out her hands to Nina, who took the baby and held her for a few moments before handing the child to Neka.

"I stand in front of you today to plead for Uloma, who has endured rape by one of the men among us," Nina said. "We have a beautiful child in front of us, yet no one claims to have fathered her. Many of you may know this man but are afraid to expose him. The crime of impregnating a mad woman is punishable by death, yet we have shunned our laws because most of our men think little of a woman's rights. Before I continue, I would like Chief Eze to affirm the punishment for this crime."

Chief Eze looked at Ada, then at Nina. He stood up from his *agada* and walked to the front of the crowd. "My people, this is a difficult day for all of us. Neka is a free woman, and we must all rejoice. Ada, on the other hand, faces death at the gorge of the oracle. On top of this, in keeping with our tradition and beliefs as handed down by our great-grandfathers, a man who impregnates a mad woman must also die at the hands of the oracle. This is an unforgivable crime; five men have been killed during my lifetime for this crime. But if someone accuses another falsely of this crime, the accuser is dealt the same fate." The chief turned and looked at Nina as he walked back to his seat, a slight smile on his face, believing that Nina would fail to prove her case. He would then seize the opportunity to free Ada. Of course, he knew there would be opposition, but he had the support of a few elders to turn the tide in Ada's favor.

"I have a set of pictures to show the people that I took of this man raping Uloma," Nina said, and handed one of the pictures to Mazi Igwe.

Mazi Igwe flinched. He could not believe his eyes, and his face twisted in surprise and horror. Looking away, he handed the picture to Chief Eze. Nina meanwhile distributed the rest of the pictures to the elders and the crowd.

"It's impossible!" Chief Eze screamed, and stormed toward Nina. "My own son! It's impossible. You are a mad woman yourself!" He was quickly restrained by Mazi Igwe, but managed to crumple the picture in his palm, and threw it violently in Nina's face. Nina remained calm, but Ada was shaking. Neka smiled slightly as her eyes met Ada's. A wave of hostility was directed from the crowd against Ada and the chief. Several of the elders joined the people as they began to voice their anger: "Kill the rapist son, kill the witch. No one is above our laws."

The chief heard it. There was panic in his eyes.

"This is absurd. Why do you want to embarrass me and my family? Is this what it is all about? No, it's impossible!" Chief Eze continued to yell. "It's impossible."

Nina turned to the elders, then to the crowd. "I have come for justice, not to seek revenge or to make false accusations."

"No one should listen to this evil woman," Chief Eze interjected. "The pictures are fake. As you all know, nowadays technology can fake anything. She made it all up. She and her foreign friends would stop at nothing to destroy our town. They are up to no good."

"I would like Chinedu, the chief's son, to come forward," Mazi Igwe said. His voice was subdued, but firm.

"No!" Chief Eze rose angrily from his seat. "I won't let my son take part in this witch hunt. Chinedu has always conducted himself honorably. He will succeed me as chief. Every one of you knows this. To stand in front of you and witness my family dragged through the mud is a dishonor I will not tolerate." Chief Eze shook with rage. He only just managed to keep himself from sagging to the ground.

Mazi Igwe looked around at everyone. "People of Eze, this must be the most difficult time in our town's history. First, there was Neka's trial, then this inquiry, which has produced such an unexpected turn. But no one is above the law. And so I must call Chinedu to answer the accusations against him. Neither Chief Eze nor the elders have the power to stop this proceeding."

"You may proceed, Nina," Mazi Igwe said, as Chinedu came up and stood in front of the people. He couldn't have been more than twenty-five. He was shorter and more muscular than his father, but with the peevish expression of those who seldom smiled. His large nose and lips gave him a slightly subhuman look. It was the first time Nina had seen him in daylight, and she disliked him more than ever.

"Thank you, Mazi Igwe." Nina looked at the elders, then at the crowd. "Chief Eze has called me a fake. I will prove to you, my kind people of Eze, that my intentions are from the heart. I was brought up a God-fearing child. My mother taught me to love and respect others, to give my heart to those in need. It is this belief that stirs me, as a human being, to fight for the underprivileged. Chief Eze and his family come from honorable people, but many changes have taken place in our town.

"First we have the woman who stands in front of you, Ada, who through fear and intrigue took advantage of our people's superstitious beliefs, and murdered our babies. While this outdated custom was halted by the government in distant towns, she convinced you that the gods wanted our twins. So many of you heard the cries of your babies in the forest, as they were eaten by soldier ants and civet cats, but you were afraid to intervene. Some cried desperately for help for days, thirsty and hungry, but we never came. And our children continue to die at her hands through female circumcision. Some of those children would have grown up to become doctors and lawyers in big cities. But one thing is clear, the chief could have stopped this madness. But he ignored Ada's crimes; he turned his back on the butchery because there was something in it for him. Or perhaps he too believed in superstition. Yet he has the effrontery to call my pictures a fake. But let me be impudent in my turn and ask him to see the marks on his son's arm."

Nina turned to Chinedu. "Pull up your left sleeve!"

Chinedu ignored Nina's command.

"Do it now!" Nina shouted. Her voice echoed over the valley.

The people looked fixedly at Chinedu, not taking their eyes from him for a moment. Chinedu looked at his father with shame and fear. He swallowed hard, then gradually pulled his left sleeve to his elbow. On his forearm were the tooth marks.

"Are those not Uloma's tooth marks?" Nina asked. "I want you to look our people in the face and tell them those are not Uloma's tooth marks."

The chief saw his son's guilt in his eyes. He knew it would be the end of his family's chieftaincy. Chinedu, his only son,.was slated to inherit the throne. But he could not save him. He had sealed his son's fate when he told the crowd the punishment for impregnating a mad woman.

"I have shamed my father and my family, whom I love with all my heart," Chinedu said. "I apologize to the elders, and to our people. I have no excuse for my actions. I hope you will find it in your hearts to forgive my crime and spare my life."

Nina was angry. Chinedu apologized to everyone, but not to Uloma, the very person he had so badly abused.

"You have no remorse for your actions, nor any conscience," she said. "I watched in horror as you brutally beat and raped this poor mad woman, and now you apologized to everyone but the one who suffered in your hands. I recommend that, for your actions, you meet the same fate as Ada."

Chief Eze stood up slowly. His face was drawn, and his eyes sunken. Though he seemed a defeated man, Nina knew he was also filled with injured pride. He spoke: "You may do as you wish with my son. But remember, I have served you as chief fairly. If you and Mazi Igwe find it in your hearts, allow my son to come home with me." With that the chief walked away.

Nina looked at Chinedu. His lips paled as he saw his father leave. He and Ada were left to face the crowd alone. The feeling that surged through Nina at that moment was a mixture of sympathy and contempt. Chinedu had just been abandoned by his own father. Ten warriors approached from behind the crowd. Suddenly the people grew quiet. The only noise that could be heard were sobs from Chinedu. The sky was clouding over and the sun had hidden behind them. A slight wind rustled against tree branches, sending leaves floating down onto the crowd. Mazi Igwe gave a deep sigh. He had never imagined he would be the one to preside over the death sentence of a future chief.

Nina, Neka, and Uloma watched as the warriors approached. Their faces were covered in the same fashion as the elders, but with an added bandana of leaves from palm frond around their heads. They seized Ada, tied her hands behind her back, and placed a blindfold over her head. She offered no resistance, as if she were resigned to her fate. As the warriors turned to Chinedu, he looked at the people with fear-filled eyes, then at Mazi Igwe, and finally at Uloma, with true remorse in his eyes, and a gesture of apology. There was such hurt in his heart that he was unable to speak. Nina saw this, but she could do nothing to stop the warriors.

The warriors led Ada and Chinedu through some narrow bushes up the sheer cliff, a tottering stairway. The crowd followed, though some remained behind in the trees for a better look. Within minutes they reached the jutting cliff. The ledge was covered with white sand and leaves, which had been blown uphill by the winds.

Ada and Chinedu were now inches from the triangular shelf, which looked down into the gorge. Chinedu shook as he heard the roaring torrent below; his cries were clearly heard despite the hood.

"Wait!" Nina shouted, as the warriors took their final step. "I have one request to make of our people. Please, find it in your hearts to spare Chinedu's life. I beg this of you."

Nina looked at Mazi Igwe. His gaze met hers. Mazi Igwe nodded to the crowd.

"I know how you must feel about his father's actions," Nina said. "They were terrible in their own way. But find it in your hearts to forgive his son. I'm sure he would feel he owed his very life to all of you, not to his father who did not stand by to bid farewell to his only son."

Nina looked at the crowd, and not a single one of them objected to the call for leniency. She turned to Uloma. Uloma nodded silently and squeezed Nina against her chest. Uloma had found forgiveness in her heart.

Most of the mothers had tears in their eyes as the warriors led Chinedu away from the sheer cliff.

"Ada!" Nina yelled over the noise from the waters that raged in the gorge beneath. Her voice was heard over the hills. "There is still time to apologize for your crimes, to be forgiven."

The sky had grown dark, and rain had begun to clatter down upon the people. "Let me be," Ada said. "I despise and hate you. My only regret is that I did not finish you off when I had the chance. You are a lucky woman. If I'm spared, I will stab you in the back at night. The world is too small for both of us." With those words, and with the warriors moving up behind her, Ada jumped. She gave a loud scream, her voice trailing off into the valley as she fell. She plummeted two hundred feet into the roaring torrent. Nina closed her eyes as the crowd gave out a loud cry.

Soaked by the rain, Nina turned to Neka and Uloma. The crowd began to disperse as the rain turned into a downpour. Some nodded their heads respectfully as they passed Nina, but her heart was leaden. She felt she could have somehow saved Ada. But in the end, Ada was a victim of her own vanity and malice.

Chinedu sat alone on a large stone, looking into space. Seeing Nina, he rose to his feet and walked shakily towards her. He was totally drenched in the rain. Nina froze.

"May I hold your hand?" Chinedu asked. Nina slowly offered her hand. "I will be forever indebted to you for giving me back my life." He then turned to Uloma, trembling with emotion and fear. "I treated you badly. I hope you will find it in your heart to forgive the wrongs I did you. You didn't deserve it. You have already suffered so much in the hands of our people."

Uloma began to cry. As Chinedu walked quietly away, he took one last look at Uloma. Now only Nina, Neka, and Uloma remained. Then Neka and Uloma also walked quietly away, leaving Nina alone.

It had stopped raining, and the sun that had disappeared behind the clouds earlier began to peek over the green hilltops. Its warmth, mingling with the dying wind, filled Nina with a soft sense of ease. Moisture from the rains hung from thick leafy bushes that grew in the folds of the cliff. Each trembling raindrop on the leaves reflected a multitude of rays from the sun. As Nina looked across the horizon, she saw that a rainbow had slung over the mist that rose from the waterfall, and the animals of the forest had resumed their quiet chanting. She knew her mother and Chichi would be proud of her, as she was of them...

*   *   *

**PLEASE HELP FIGHT FEMALE
CIRCUMCISION AROUND THE WORLD.**

Send Donations To:
Trident Media Women Education Fund
801 N Pitt Street, Suite 123
Alexandria, VA 22314 USA
703-684-6895

The Women of Eze

by

Sam Asinugo

Available at your local bookstore or use this page to order.

0-9707954-1-6 Women of Eze - $12.75 U.S / $17.00 in Canada

Send to: Trident Media Inc.

801 N. Pitt Street, Suite 123

Alexandria, VA 22314 USA

#1-877-874-6334

Please send me the items I have checked above. I am enclosing $_____(please add $3.50 per book to cover postage and handling). Send check, money order, or credit card.

Card #_____ Exp. date _____

Mr./Mrs./Ms._____

Address_____

City/State_____Zip_____

Please allow one week for delivery.
Prices and availabilty subject to change without notice.

Printed in the United States
4077